TEXAS ROSE EVERMORE

A TEXAS ROSE RANCH NOVEL
BOOK 3

KATIE GRAYKOWSKI

INTRODUCTION

From International Bestselling Author Katie Graykowski comes a love story about love, laughter, and ranching.

Rosie Gomez is an event planner with a wedding to plan and nothing or no one will stand in her way. She has moved into a cottage at the Texas Rose Ranch, but ranch life doesn't really suit her. Her high heels sink into the mud, her cell phone only works in one square foot of the cottage, there are mosquitos the size of VW Beetles, and Dallas Rose—third son of the Texas Rose Ranch—treats her like she has the plague. She can't wait to get back to Austin.

Dallas Rose can't get Rosie Gomez out of his mind. She's a straight-talking city-girl who doesn't belong on the ranch, but somehow, she fits right in. The minute he laid eyes on her, he knew she was the girl for him. Unfortunately, whenever he sees her, his mouth stops working.

Can he convince her to take a chance on love and make the ranch her home?

Fans of Susan Elizabeth Phillips and Rachel Gibson won't want to miss this story full of laughter, love, and ranching.

ALSO BY KATIE GRAYKOWSKI

THE FORT WORTH WRANGLERS

Lyric and Lingerie http://amzn.to/2BRYJFH

Harmony and High Heels http://amzn.to/2ETbdj7

THE TOUGH LADIES

Cold As January https://amzn.to/2HxqXJS

Sweet Susie Sweet https://amzn.to/2JL8hTj

THE CHRISTMAS NETWORK

Welcome To Christmas, Texas https://amzn.to/2BIyETJ

Return to Christmas, Texas https://amzn.to/2Ri7Oi5

A Christmas Network Box Set Books 1-2 https://amzn.to/3oSUtMh

Mystery

PTO MURDER CLUB

Rest In Pieces http://amzn.to/2CJrxNz

Blown To Pieces http://amzn.to/2EVjm6U

Just One Piece http://amzn.to/2FxKiX9

Bits and Pieces https://amzn.to/37zY9sC

Box Set Books 1-4 https://amzn.to/3mO9hKh

Urban Fantasy Sci-Fi

TIME, INC.

The Navigator -Out Soon

For Denise Howell—good friend, sometimes coworker, and Black Friday shopping guru. Move back to Texas soon. I miss you.

1

Rosie Gomez was a woman on a mission. She had a wedding to plan, and nothing or no one would stand in her way. This was her coup de grace, her swan song, her last large-scale event in her event-planning career. It would be perfect or by God she'd die trying.

The Texas Rose Ranch—second largest ranch in Texas—was a wonderful backdrop for an outdoor wedding, only it was remote... and well... remote.

Rosie smoothed out imaginary wrinkles on her red business suit and stepped out onto the front lawn of the house of her best friend, CanDee McCain, soon to be CanDee Rose. The icepick heels of Rosie's Loubies—bought secondhand off of eBay—sank into the grass as she pulled out her tape measure and measured the distance between the front porch and a large clump of oak trees.

Behind her, a mechanical buzzing noise signaled that her other best friend, Justus Rose, was headed this way. Rosie turned around and shaded her eyes from the April sunshine. Justus rode up the driveway behind the wheel of a Bobcat. She was the best landscape architect in the business, and she was in the middle of renovating CanDee's front yard.

Justus parked next to Rosie, turned off the Bobcat, and lifted the cage door that kept her from getting hurt. "You really should invest in some boots."

"I have lots of boots. Their heels would sink into the ground too." A professional dressed as a professional should, and that included heels even when she was traipsing through a cow pasture. She didn't make the rules.

Justus shot her a yeah-right look. "Work boots. You need work boots."

"All of my work boots have heels." Her oldest sister had drummed "Dress for the job you want and not the job you have" into her head from an early age. Only, now that she thought about it, managing the new Texas Rose Ranch Bed-and-Breakfast probably did require ugly work boots. She glanced at Justus's lace-up, man-style work boots. Rosie mashed her lips together. Over her dead body was she wearing those. As a woman, there were four things she wouldn't compromise on—getting equal pay for women, stopping domestic violence, ending childhood hunger, and not wearing ugly shoes. Those were the four pillars on which she'd built her life and she wasn't about to change now.

Justus held her leg up so Rosie could inspect her mud-spackled boots. "Trust me, your feet will thank you."

Rosie's toes recoiled in disgust.

"They're even worse up close." She shook her head. "I'm good."

"Don't knock them until you've tried them." Justus unrolled a set of landscape plans. "You need to sign off on these because I'm starting the demo today. AG is with her father. Rowdy read another baby-rearing book and he's dying to prove to the world that he knows everything about babies."

Rowdy, second oldest son of the Texas Rose Ranch family and a master vintner, was Justus's new husband. Their seven-year-old son, Hugh, wasn't happy that two months ago his mother had given birth to a baby girl—AG, short for Anna-Grace.

"Maybe I'll stop by the winery and give Hugh and AG a kiss." Rosie had been in and out of the ranch weekly for the last year. Now she was moving here permanently. Or she would be once her bags that were still in her car were unpacked in the rustic cottage turned guesthouse. Taking a leap of faith and investing all of her savings in the Texas Rose Ranch Bed-and-Breakfast was the first truly risky thing she'd ever done. And now she was part owner and the full-time manager.

Justus grinned from ear to ear. "The whole ranch has baby fever. AG has more uncles than she knows what to do with."

"That's because she's the cutest baby in the world." Rosie wasn't biased. It was true.

"Rowdy's convinced she's a genius and that the gibberish she's begun to babble is in fact Mandarin Chinese." Justus pointed to the landscape plans. "Are you sure you want a waterfall right there?"

"Do you have a better idea?" The wedding was less than two months away. Every single change would cost her precious time.

Justus pointed to the space next to a copse of trees. "Putting it right there makes it look like it was always a part of the landscape."

Rosie stared at the spot and readjusted her mental image of the layout for the ceremony. If she moved three of the tables to the other side of the yard, then the waterfall could go there. She had to remember that this was CanDee's front yard, and CanDee had to live with it after the wedding. "You're right, it would look much better between those trees."

"I'm glad you agree." Justus threw her an over-bright smile. "Because we need to discuss these rose bushes." She pointed to a line of bushes on the plans.

"What's wrong with the rose bushes?" They would scent the air, as well as give lots of pops of color.

"They're lined up in perfect little rows like crops waiting to be harvested." Justus ran her finger along the line of roses.

"Yes, and that's a problem why?" Rosie's life worked better with everything lined up in little rows.

"Because nature doesn't do symmetrical rows. In two years, the canes of the roses will completely overtake the front porch and the gazebo." Justus pointed to the area that hopefully by next week would have the gazebo.

"How do we fix that?" Rosie knew that she needed to think long-term for this front yard, but she was having a hard time seeing the yard through the forest of wedding plans.

Justus but an arm around Rosie's shoulders. "Remember that time in college when we spent that weekend volunteering at the at-risk-teen camp and they did all of those trust exercises?"

"Yes. Having to free-fall back off of a platform and trust that the others were going to catch me was literally my worst nightmare." Rosie shivered at the memory. It wasn't that she didn't trust total strangers to catch her, it was more that she was a control freak and couldn't control the situation. Realization dawned. "Oh God, you're going to toss my plans and ask me to trust you."

Justus's smile turned used-car-salesman bright. "Don't worry. I'm going to catch you, unlike those ungrateful kids at that stupid camp. Who knew that you could actually break your tailbone?"

"I had to sit on that dumb donut pillow for weeks." Rosie's palms began to sweat. "It's not that I don't trust you, because you know I totally trust you with my life, but ..."

Just because she trusted someone with her life, didn't mean that she trusted them with her work.

She glanced at the landscape plans. This was her final wedding. It had to be perfect.

"I think you need to sit down. Your face is turning this awful shade of mint green." Justus led her to the front steps. "Just put your head between your knees until the nausea passes."

"No, I'm fine. I'm good." Rosie put her head between her knees anyway.

"I know you're a crazy control freak, but you're going to have to trust me on this." Justus patted her back.

"'You're going to have to trust me on this.' Words every control freak never wants to hear." The nausea was beginning to pass. On her very first wedding job, she'd trusted the cake maker to interpret the beachy theme of the wedding. It had been a disaster. The cake had been neon blue with plastic seashells all over it. Rosie had thrown together some cream cheese frosting and slapped it on the cake. Luckily, the bride and groom had loved the minimalist beach vibe she hadn't known she was going for.

"Come on, you can do it." Justus hip-bumped her. "Walk out on the ledge and take that leap of faith."

"You know I'm afraid of heights." Life would be so much

easier if she could just delegate everything and not have to do anything herself, but she couldn't work that way, and she wasn't interested in changing anytime soon.

"Would it make you feel better if I drew up some plans and had you sign off on them?" Justus patted her back one more time and then stood and made her way to the Bobcat. She pulled out a second set of plans. "Well, what do you know? I happen to have a second set of plans right here."

"Funny how that worked out." Rosie sat up.

Justus rolled them out on the front porch. "I even colored them in so you'll get a feel for how the plants work together."

Rosie studied the plans. "I like how you moved the roses to the middle but still left room for the walkway." Damn, these were way better than her plans. She leaned in closer to get a better look. "What are the plants lining the walkways?"

"Lavender. It gives off a nice scent, has pretty purple flowers, and it repels mosquitoes." Justus ran her finger along the walkways. "I've also incorporated lemon thyme and rosemary for added bug protection."

"Any mosquito with an ounce of self-preservation wouldn't dare show up to one of my events."

"On the off chance that mosquito HQ didn't get the word out to all of their bloodsucking membership, I think we should go all backup plan with the herbs." Justus pointed to the new waterfall. She'd toned down the height and made the pond beneath much wider. It looked like it had been there since God populated the earth.

"I like it." It was hard for Rosie to relinquish control, but on rare occasions it needed to be done. She swallowed down the jaw-dropping fear and nodded. "Go for it."

"Really, just like that? I thought there'd been some

yelling, or at least some vomiting." Justus sounded disappointed. "I'd blocked off most of my morning just to talk you down off of the ledge. It's kind of a letdown."

"What's kind of a letdown?" CanDee opened the front door.

"She just okayed the new plans." Justus stared into Rosie's eyes. "Are you high?"

CanDee laugh-snorted. "If you really think Rosie's high, I'm going to need to see your eyes, because I'm thinking that you're high."

Justus widened her eyes like Bela Lugosi and said in her cheesiest Dracula impression, "Look into my eyes."

"Please, that was a terrible Bela Lugosi impression." Rosie widened her eyes. "Look into my eyes."

Justus stuck out her tongue. "Okay, fine, yours really is better. Damn your Hispanic accent. You sound just like him."

"I thought he was Hungarian." CanDee sat down beside Rosie.

"Yes, but he sounds Hispanic." Justus rolled up the plans and shook her head. "She just signed off on them. No hassle."

"That's a shame. We had this whole plan. It involved tears and pleading and finally threats of violence." CanDee shook her head. "Total letdown." She grinned broadly. "I do take comfort in the fantastic morning sex I just had."

Justus reached around Rosie and high-fived CanDee. "I partook in the same thing this morning."

"I hate both of you." Rosie hadn't been on a date, much less had sex, in over a year.

"There are plenty of men around here. You should pick one." Justus gestured to the man-free front yard.

"Yes, I can see that they're beating down my door." Rosie

stood and brushed off the dirt from her bottom. "Perhaps they're all at the cottage now. I'd better run home and check."

She was kidding, and they knew her well enough to know that.

"I thought you were going to talk to her about work boots." CanDee pointed to Rosie's red Loubies.

"I did, and she rejected them like a tent revival preacher casts out Satan." Justus threw up her hands. "I've done all I can."

"I don't see you wearing work boots." Rosie pointed to CanDee's strappy-sandal-clad feet.

"I'm not on my feet all the time. I'm a writer. We live the soft life. My morning commute consists of walking from the coffeepot to my home office." Her eyes scrunched up and she tapped her index finger against her pursed lips. "Come to think of it, I should just move the coffeepot into my office. That way I don't have to walk anywhere."

"That's just lazy." Justus shook her head. "And sad."

"Lazy is such an ugly word. I prefer efficient." CanDee stood and stretched. "I'm headed to town for seven crates of sticky notes and enough blue Jell-O to suspend Lefty's boots in. Need anything?"

CanDee and an old ranch hand named Lefty had a hate/hate relationship that involved lots of practical jokes and smack talk. Rosie shrugged. Everyone needed a hobby.

"No, I think I'm good." Rosie made her way to the golf cart Lefty had assigned to her. She'd passed both his written and oral driving tests with flying colors, but it had been her relationship with Justus that had won the old ranch hand over. Simply put, he loved Justus and thought CanDee was Satan's sassy stepsister.

CanDee frowned at Rosie's golf cart. "Kiss-ass."

CanDee had been permanently banned from using all machines owned by the Texas Rose Ranch, but she stole one from time-to-time just to piss off Lefty. Once, Rosie had heard that CanDee had taken his prized vintage tractor on a joy ride.

Rosie put her hand over her heart, mortally wounded. "I'm not a kiss-ass. I'm the teacher's pet. Get your suck-ups right."

Justus blew CanDee a kiss. "I'm the kiss-ass." She pointed to the Bobcat. "I get to play with the big-boy machines."

The Bobcat was covered in mud, and Rosie's second worst nightmare involved being covered in mud. "Better you than me. I like the girly-girl machines. I'm holding out for the Bobcat that has unicorns and rainbows painted on it."

Justus glanced at CanDee. "Remind me why we're friends with her?"

"Because she can talk her way out of anything. Remember when she talked that sheriff's deputy out of giving us a ticket for going eighty in a fifty-five?" CanDee smiled to herself. "What was the excuse she used?"

"I told him that my hair dryer was broken and we had to drive fast with all the windows down because I had a very important job interview." Rosie was rather proud of her ability to talk her way out of things.

"Classic Rosie." Justus climbed into the Bobcat and pulled the door closed.

Rosie slid behind the wheel of her golf cart. She waved goodbye to both CanDee and Justus. Justus was about to tear up the front yard. If Rosie was being honest with herself, and she usually was, she just couldn't take that much mess. Clutter was like nails on a chalkboard, while destruction simply made her sick. She was woman enough to know her weaknesses.

Plus, she had her own mess of sorts to clean up. She'd left her bags packed in her car. There was a part of her that was ashamed of the fact that all that baggage had been weighing on her. Perfectionism had its drawbacks.

2

Dallas Rose wasn't exactly spying on them. He was just eavesdropping on the side of the house. He'd spent the better part of an hour working up the courage to finally speak to Rosie, and he hadn't been able to even step out of the shadows.

Love sucked.

At least, he was pretty sure it was love. Last year, when Rosie had walked in to his older brother's kitchen, Dallas had taken one look at her and known she was the girl for him. Unfortunately, when he was around her, his tongue tied in knots that would make an Eagle Scout proud.

"Is there a reason you're lurking around the side of my house?" It was his older brother Cinco.

Dallas turned around to find him leaning against the side of the house.

"I was just ..." He had nothing.

"You're not some sort of Peeping Tom, are you? Since you're my brother and all, I won't turn you in to the sheriff, but I'm going to have to beat the crap out of you." Cinco shrugged one shoulder. "I'm sure Mom will understand."

"I'm not peeping in your windows. I was just ..." Still had nothing.

"Working up the courage to finally talk to Rosie?" A watermelon-slice smile broke out on his brother's lips.

"No." Yes. "I was just ..."

"Right, you were just ..." Cinco continued to smile. "I know you have a crush on Rosie. Everyone but Rosie knows it. Every time you see her, your face turns all red like you're having a stroke and incoherent words fall out of your mouth. It's hilarious."

"I don't know what you're talking about." Dallas had never had a problem talking to women. His twin brother, Worth, was the shy one. Dallas was the extrovert. At least, he had been until Rosie came along. Now Worth was the chatty one, and Dallas lurked on the side of houses just to get a glimpse of her.

"Where's all of the Rose charm? Once, you told me you could have any woman you chose, only you didn't want to choose because it was bound to make all the other women so sad." Cinco's shoulders shook with laughter.

"I was eighteen and stupid. Are you happy now? I'm finally admitting it." Ten years ago he'd made one stupid comment, and the world would never let him live it down. "Thanks for all of the brotherly support."

"Brotherly support? You've been watching too much *Dr. Phil*. As your older brother, my job is to pound on you from time to time to remind you of your total insignificance in the world. Also, advice offering is part of the deal, but the beating you up is way more fun." Cinco really was enjoying his discomfort.

"I hope we've entered the advice part of your brotherly job, because I've been taking an online kickboxing class and I can kill you with nothing but my elbow and my left ring finger." True, the online course wasn't as good as taking it in person, but the ranch was a good hour and a half away from the closest gym.

"Advice it is. Don't take any wooden nickels. A penny saved is a penny earned. Don't get your nose pierced during allergy season. CanDee told me that last one," Cinco said. "Seems reasonable."

Just once, Dallas wanted to be taken seriously by his brothers. "Thanks." The "screw you" was implied.

"You're welcome. Feel free to come to me anytime for advice." Cinco turned on his heel and headed toward his pickup. "Nice talk."

"The pleasure was all yours." Dallas rolled his eyes. Sometimes there was way too much family around.

"When are you going to ask her out?" Justus yelled over the Bobcat's engine. She pulled the Bobcat alongside him and shut off the engine.

Yep, way too much family. "Good God, is nothing private?"

"Nope." Justus just grinned. "She's single and has been for a long time. You should snatch her up before someone else does."

"Who else?" Rosie was his woman, whether she knew it or not. "I need names."

"Somebody's jealous," Justus sing-songed.

"I am not." He totally was. "I just think that with her living here now, the ranch hands should leave her alone. Mixing business and pleasure is a bad idea."

"Isn't that would you'd like to do?" Justus was fast becoming that annoying sister he'd never wanted.

"That's different." He wasn't sure how, but it was.

"Yep, I can see that." She smiled up at him expectantly.

"What? Did you come back here just to give me a hard

time?" With over eight hundred thousand acres, he should be able to get a little alone time, but no, he couldn't throw a rock without hitting a family member.

She pointed to the ground at his feet. "You're standing where I need to dig."

"Oh. Sorry." He stepped out of the way. "Seriously, though, have you heard anything about someone else asking her out?"

Competition had never been a problem before. What if Rosie preferred someone else's company to his?

"No. Would you like me to pass her a note in the cafeteria at lunch?" Justus fired up the Bobcat. "You should lock her down before someone else steps in."

He knew it, but he was at a loss for how to make it happen. He'd never had trouble talking to women before. This sucked.

Justus stuck her hand out of the cage and pointed to the golf cart pulling into the driveway. "I swiped her phone so she'd have to come back." She gave him a thumbs-up. "You're welcome."

She drove off behind the house.

Oh, crap, Rosie was back. Should he wait for her casually on the porch? Or maybe he'd just lean against the porch. Or should he walk around the side of the house and pretend he'd just walked up? But what reason would he have for being here? He swallowed down the saliva pooling in his mouth. This was a disaster.

She waved and his heart rate kicked up a notch.

Then reality crashed down on him. She knew he was here, so a casual stop-by was out of the question. It was a full minute before he remembered to wave back. Since he'd taken so long, it was awkward.

She pulled up right in front of him. The red color of her suit looked really pretty against her skin.

She smiled up at him.

He stared down at her, his mind going blank.

She continued to smile at him, like she was waiting for him to do something. He just stared and stared and stared.

"Okay then. I'm just here for my phone." She shook her head and stepped out of the golf cart. She shaded her eyes from the sun and scanned the porch, looking for her phone. She picked it up and waved it at him. "Found it."

He opened his mouth to tell her how beautiful she was, but the only thing that came out was, "Justus stole your phone so I'd get a chance to talk to you." He said it very fast and all in one breath.

Her eyes screwed up as she watched him carefully. "Okay. Why?"

He waited for words to spring out of his mouth, but nothing happened.

Rosie slid the phone into her suit pocket and then crossed her arms over her chest. "Have I done something to you?"

No, but he'd sure as hell love to do something to her, like ripping that conservative red suit off so he could memorize every square inch of her body. He felt his eyes go huge. Had he said that out loud?

His eyes went to her face. Surely, if he'd said it out loud she'd be mad or, well... madder. She looked kinda pissed right now.

"Huh?" was all he could get to come out of his mouth.

"Have I offended you in some way, because you go out of your way to avoid me." She smiled as she held her hand out for him to shake. "Let's start over. I'm Rosie Gomez. It's nice to meet you, Dallas Rose."

He stared at her hand, but he couldn't quite figure out how to make his hand take hers. He glanced down at his hand, but it still wouldn't move.

Finally, she yanked her hand back. "Whatever I've done, I apologize."

He watched her turn around and march right back to the golf cart.

Until now, he hadn't thought it was possible to make the situation worse, but things on her end had gone from awkward to animosity in no time flat.

He wanted to run after her, but his feet had stopped working. Talk about things not working. How were they supposed to ride off into the sunset together when he turned mute every time he saw her? Maybe he should learn sign language. He glanced down at his hands. That wouldn't help since they seemed to be broken too.

"That was pathetic," Worth called from behind a large oak tree. He waggled his phone. "Thank God I got that up on Instagram. It was a miracle, considering I only have half a bar."

"You better be kidding." Dallas grabbed the phone from his twin brother and checked his Instagram timeline. Sure enough, there was a video of him trying to talk to Rosie. It really was pathetic. "Ten years ago, I'd have beat you to death over this, but look how much I've grown."

Dallas's right fist shot out and smashed against Worth's jaw. And it was on. Worth tackled Dallas and got a few good ones into the kidneys. Dallas tripped Worth, who landed flat on his back. It was time to ground and pound. Dallas pummeled him with his fists.

Ice-cold water doused his back, and he practically jumped a foot in the air. He rolled off Worth to find Rosie holding a garden hose and staring down at him.

"Are you crazy?" She tossed the hose down and went to Worth. She knelt beside him. "He's hurt."

"He'll be okay." How about that? An actual, intelligent sentence had popped out of his mouth. He grinned from ear to ear. There was hope yet.

She helped Worth up. "Have both of you lost your minds?"

"This really isn't a big deal. We do this all the time." Worth rubbed his jaw.

"What in God's name for?" She looked honestly horrified.

"It's a sibling thing." Worth shook it off. "We fight... a lot."

"I have three older sisters, and I can say that we never roll around on the front lawn trying to beat each other to death." Rosie's tone said she wasn't buying it.

She glared down at Dallas. "It's one thing for you to ignore me, but to beat on your poor brother? You should be ashamed of yourself."

His mouth had gone back to not working.

Worth moaned and grabbed his side. "Think you could help me back to my house?"

She patted his back. "You bet."

Worth turned around and discreetly stuck out his tongue at Dallas.

Dallas had never hated his brother more.

Holy crap, was Worth interested in Rosie too?

It wouldn't be the first time they'd liked the same girl. But it was the first time Worth had out charmed him. Usually, Worth was the shy, awkward one. This tables-turning thing sucked.

If Worth was interested in Rosie, surely, he would have said something. Dallas rolled to his feet. This was just another way that his younger-by-two-minutes brother was punishing him for being born first.

He rolled his eyes. Family was always trouble, and with one as big as his, there was always someone around to film that trouble and post it on Instagram.

What was he supposed to do now? His best friend/worst enemy was being pampered and taken care of by the woman Dallas wanted.

He'd never not been able to charm a woman before. This didn't make sense. He was the comic relief in the family, and now he could barely get out a sentence that contained both a subject and a verb. Had he had a love-induced lobotomy while he wasn't looking? Surely he would have noticed someone poking around in his brain.

Or maybe he'd been abducted by aliens? He had seen lots of weird flashing lights at night. True, most of them were fireflies, but still. He wasn't ruling out alien abduction as a reason for his lapses in motor and verbal function.

Or it might have been all of the punches he'd taken from his brothers. Yep, that was probably it. And now the perpetrator of most of those punches was going out of his way to make Dallas jealous. Again, family was trouble.

Dallas had walked over instead of driving, and now he was thankful for that. He needed to walk off the embarrassment and the frustration of this morning.

He did take comfort in the fact that things really couldn't get worse.

3

The next night Rosie, CanDee, Justus, and Lucy were having girls' night at Justus's house. No boys allowed. Lately, Rosie had been so busy tying up loose ends so she could move to the Texas Rose that she'd neglected girl time.

"What do you think of Dallas?" CanDee popped a Double Stuf Oreo in her mouth and smiled like she'd just tasted heaven.

"It's a fun town." Rosie snuggled a sleeping AG up higher on her shoulder. The weight of a sleeping baby felt good.

"She meant the person." Lucy, matriarch of the Rose clan and mother to Cinco, Rowdy, Dallas, Worth, and T-Bone, tossed back a handful of Peanut M&M's.

"Oh. Um... he seems nice... I guess." How did she say politely to his mother that he was an ass?

"I think you make him nervous." Justus dropped a kiss on her daughter's head.

CanDee used her extra-long leg to reach around Rosie and kick Justus in the shin.

There was something going on here that Rosie didn't understand.

"What do you mean?" The only people Rosie ever remembered making nervous were venders who didn't live up to the promises they'd made her. Come to think of it, nervous wasn't the right word. After she got through with them, terrified fit their state of mind so much better.

Everyone fell silent.

"I don't understand. What's going on here that I don't know about?" Was there some sort of inside joke?

"Nothing." Lucy cleared her throat. "I think Dallas is a little intimidated by you."

"Really? Because I think he hates me. He treats me like an ex-girlfriend who loaned him money. When he's not avoiding me, he's glaring at me." She was pretty sure it was hatred and not intimidation that Dallas felt for her. She shook her head. "I can't think of anything I've done to make him angry."

Then again, people had remarked in the past that she did tend to steamroll over them, and sometimes that made them angry. But she didn't remember steamrolling anyone recently.

"Trust me, he's not angry," Lucy said. "He likes you."

"What was with the fight I broke up yesterday?" Rosie had never had to break up a fight. Well, except for a catfight or two. That's where she'd learned to turn the hose on them.

Lucy waved like it was no big deal. "They do that a lot."

"Why?" Rosie and her sisters yelled at each other, but it had never gotten to bloodshed. True, it had gotten close, but still, no one had ever had to go to the hospital, and rarely did body parts need to be iced down.

Lucy shrugged. "They're men. I can offer no other explanation."

CanDee hip-bumped Rosie. "She's right. I didn't grow up with siblings, so this whole fighting family thing is new to me, but I've seen all of the brothers fight. It's just horseplay. They don't do any real damage. You have sisters, surely it's the same."

"Rarely do we try to kill each other. Well, except when Esther made tamales a couple of Christmas Eves ago. We all ended up in the ER. Esther's good at so many things, but cooking isn't one of them. Our lives would all be so much better if she gave up on it." No one could call her sister a quitter, because she still cooked dinner every Thursday. It was odd, Rosie and her other sisters always had something else to do on Thursday night.

Justus grabbed a handful of Peanut M&M's. "Siblings are interesting. Remember that VW commercial a few years ago where the guy goes up to the car and licks the handle?"

Lucy shook her head. "No."

"Well, there was a commercial where all of these people wanted to buy this one car and a man runs up to the door and licks the handle and everyone backs away from it." CanDee pointed at Rosie. "She had to explain it to us. You know, lick it and it's yours."

"Oh, yes. I can see how if you didn't grow up with siblings, that commercial wouldn't make any sense." Lucy dug into the Peanut M&M's. "Bear's an only child. I had to explain to him the universal law of finders keepers, losers weepers."

Bear was Lucy's husband, and he was indeed a big bear of a man, but he was a gentle giant with kind eyes and a ready smile.

"I can see how things like that would be hard for an only child to understand," Rosie said. "Personally, I've fantasized about being an only child for most of my life." But if she'd been an only child, she probably would have ended up in foster care after her mother decided she was tired of being a mother and left Rosie with a neighbor and never came back. That might have happened anyway, if her mother hadn't died. Intellectually, Rosie knew she wasn't the reason for her mother's heart attack, but the frightened and heartbroken ten-year-old girl still lived inside of her, and she knew her mother had died because Rosie was a bad child. Her only apology to her sisters for their mother's death had been to work harder and longer and smarter, so they wouldn't know it was all Rosie's fault.

Her oldest sister, Louisa, who'd been twenty-two at the time, had moved her three younger sisters into her one-bedroom apartment, and somehow they'd made ends meet.

"Don't say that." CanDee put her arm around Rosie. "I love your sisters." She turned to Lucy. "She was raised by her older sisters. They started Fantastic Flans out of that one-room-apartment kitchen."

"Oh my God." Lucy's mouth fell open. "Their chocolate flan is the best thing I've ever tasted. I can't believe I'm going to admit this, but I ate all four of the chocolate flan cups in the family pack in one sitting last week. When our housekeeper, Mary, asked about it, I totally threw my sons under the bus and blamed them." She shook her head. "It may make me a terrible mother, but I don't care. It was worth it."

"They worked on that recipe for close to three years before they perfected it." Rosie couldn't help but smile. Louisa and Ariana made a good living off of their home-made flan, and so did Esther in a roundabout way. She was head of marketing.

"You should taste the coconut flan. I don't even like coconut that much, but I love their coconut flan." CanDee fanned herself like she was talking about the best sex ever. "So yummy."

"I don't think the coconut has hit the market yet." With the wedding and building the bed-and-breakfast, Rosie wasn't in the loop when it came to her sisters' business.

"Sounds wonderful. I can't wait to try it." Lucy sounded like she really meant it and not like she was just saying it.

Over the last year, Rosie had come to know that Lucy shot straight from the hip, even if she occasionally put someone's eye out.

"Back to Dallas." Gently, Justus lifted her sleeping daughter out of Rosie's arms. "I think he's cute. Don't you think he's cute?"

"Sure." What else was Rosie supposed to say? His mother and sisters-in-law were currently staring at her.

Now that she thought about it, he was kinda cute, in a Superman—dark hair and baby-blue eyes—kind of way. Also, the killer dimples on both cheeks didn't hurt. And he had a nice butt. Okay, she was willing to admit that she'd noticed his good looks a time or two. There was nothing wrong with appreciating a nice-looking man. They did it to women all the time.

"By the look on your face, I'd say that 'sure' doesn't cover it. You think he's cute." CanDee hip-bumped her again. "It's okay, it's just us girls here."

"I won't tell." Lucy crossed her heart, zipped her lips, and threw away the key.

"Okay, I'm willing to admit that I might have checked him out a couple of times. He's nice to look at... so sue me." They weren't going to let her off easy. And it didn't matter that she was attracted to Dallas. He most definitely was not attracted to her. It was funny, Worth was Dallas's identical twin, but she only felt brotherly affection for him. When they were identical twins, how could she be attracted to one but not the other?

Just because they had the same DNA didn't mean they were the same person.

"I think you should give Dallas a chance. He's a good guy." CanDee shoved another Oreo into her mouth.

"Sure, why not?" Rosie didn't know what exactly was going on here, but there wasn't a chance in hell that she and Dallas would ever have anything more than animosity between them. The fact that he was cute was beside the point.

Lucy sat up. "Now that that's settled, let's talk about the bed-and-breakfast. Do you really think we should open before the restaurant is up and running?"

Lucy, CanDee, Justus, and Rosie had all put up equal money to build the B&B. They were equal partners who voted on and discussed everything.

"I've been giving that some thought," Rosie said. "I'll take care of breakfast, and we can stock the fridge with sandwich-making items or suggest that the guests eat out while they're sightseeing in Roseville or Fredericksburg. But dinner has always been an issue. I was thinking we could hire different celebrity chefs to cook dinner. Maybe even make it a cooking class where the chef teaches the guests while they all cook dinner." She thought about it for a minute. "We could market it as a culinary getaway and include Texas Rose wines."

"That's brilliant." CanDee clapped her hands. "I would have never thought of it."

Justus held her hand up for a high five. "Rowdy loves showcasing his wines, and I love baking."

"I'd volunteer to help cook too, but the nearest hospital is like forty-five minutes away and I'm not sure EMS has enough ambulances to transport all of the food-poisoning victims before the salmonella I accidentally gave them does a number on their intestinal tracts." CanDee shrugged one shoulder. "Unless I make my famous pancakes or my meatloaf. The meatloaf only made one person sick, but that was years ago." She waved it away like it was a nonissue. "I'm pretty sure that pancakes can't kill anyone, or they haven't yet."

"Why don't you leave the cooking to those of us who haven't sent anyone to the hospital?" Rosie patted CanDee's knee. "Nothing ruins a business quite like food poisoning."

"You can help out in other ways." Lucy scooped up her granddaughter and positioned her on her shoulder. She patted the sleeping child's back. "I'm so glad we have a granddaughter. It's about time we had some girl babies." She smiled at Justus. "Did you show Rosie and CanDee what Dallas bought AG?"

"No, I forgot." Justus walked down the hall, presumably to AG's room. A couple of minutes later she stepped into the living room holding a frilly, pale-pink organza dress complete with petticoats, matching shoes, and a pink bow headband large enough to staunch a massive head wound. "Her uncles spoil her rotten."

Rosie studied the outfit. It was cute and girly and not what she'd expected. "I thought it would be a pair of cowboy boots."

There she went again stereotyping people.

"You'd think so, but all of her uncles have showered her with super frilly, girly gifts. They want to dress her up in poufy pink dresses and black patent-leather Mary Janes. It's hilarious." Justus set the outfit down on the coffee table. "Worth bought her a red rain slicker with ladybugs all over it and matching ladybug rain boots. They're so huge that she won't be able to wear them until she's ten, but they really are adorable."

"Cinco bought her the tiniest high-heel shoes. She won't be able to wear them for years, but he doesn't care." CanDee pulled one knee up and rested her chin on it. "It's so funny. He loves AG so much, but he doesn't want to hold her because he's afraid he'll break her." She glanced at Lucy. "He needs to get over it, because in seven-ish months, he's going to have one of his own."

CanDee sat back and watched the aftermath of the verbal grenade she'd just dropped.

"Oh my God, you're pregnant?" Lucy's eyes turned huge. "You're going to have a baby?"

"Yes, I've done several pregnancy tests and they're all positive." CanDee smiled from ear to ear. "I haven't told Cinco yet because what with his past relationship, I wanted to make sure."

"What happened to him?" Rosie knew Cinco had been married before, but she didn't know any of the details.

Lucy's face screwed up like she'd just smelled the world's stinkiest cheese. "His first wife lied about being pregnant so he'd marry her."

"Wow, what a bitch." Rosie rarely used the B-word, but when the bitch-hat fit, she had to call it.

"I know, right?" Justus threw an arm around CanDee and hugged her tight.

"I'm so excited." Lucy hugged her granddaughter to her. "This little one needs cousins. Lots of them. Okay, you need a blood test. I can draw your blood and take it to the hospital tomorrow. I'll have the results in minutes."

"That would be awesome." Excitement radiated off of CanDee in waves. "I can't wait to tell him." She took a deep breath and looked to be judging her words carefully. "I'd like to be able to show him the results of the blood test, or at least have you talk to him to confirm the results." She hugged Lucy. "I'd like for him to know that I'm really pregnant."

"He knows you're not like his first wife." Lucy patted her on the back.

"I know, but think about it from his perspective. He's got to have some lingering doubts, and rightfully so." CanDee had the enviable ability to see a situation from all angles.

Rosie didn't suffer from fair judgement like CanDee. She didn't see all the angles, or really want to see any other side besides her own. It wasn't stubbornness or a lack of empathy, it was more a single-minded drive to accomplish whatever she'd set out to accomplish.

Even if that accomplishment was something impossible. Like having a normal conversation with Dallas.

4

The next morning, Dallas held his nephew Hugh's
hand as they walked over to the granite quarry.
Worth was in charge of the quarry and hardly ever
blew things up for fun, but Dallas had been working on his
old-lady-stick-up-his-ass twin. This morning they were
going to have some fun.

Hell, if Dallas had been in charge of the quarry, he'd
never get any work done because he'd be blowing stuff up
all the time. That was probably why he was in charge of the
twenty-thousand-acre exotic-animal ranch and the deer-
hunting leases. People paid a pretty penny for the privilege
to hunt deer on the Texas Rose Ranch.

"Now remember, if anyone asks, we're off shooting firecrackers." Dallas didn't condone lying per se, but a little
creative truth never hurt anyone. And there were some
things that shouldn't be shared with any parental-type
people.

"Got it, Uncle Dallas. Firecrackers." The kid would have
saluted if he'd known how. He was eight going on thirty.

Dallas had never met a more serious kid. "Did you know that when hippos are upset their sweat turns red?"

Hugh loved him some random facts.

"I did not know that. Maybe I'll just get me a hippo and see for myself." Dallas didn't know much about hippo husbandry, but he was pretty sure he could get an import license for one and add him—or to be fair, her—to the exotic ranch.

"Also, billy goats pee on their own head so they can attract females." Hugh expelled random facts like other people expelled carbon dioxide.

Dallas thought about it for a minute. "Not sure how the physics involved work out. I couldn't pee on my head if I tried."

"I know. I tried in the shower, but it didn't work." Hugh sounded really disappointed. "Don't tell my mom."

Dallas held out his pinkie. "Pinkie swear I won't."

Hugh hooked pinkies with Dallas and then let go.

"Even if you did tell her, she wouldn't listen. She spends all of her time with AG." Hugh's mouth curled up in annoyance.

"That's because AG is little and needs your mother. You're practically all grown-up and don't need her as much." Dallas could see there was more than a little jealousy going on here. "You know, if you helped her out with AG, she might have more free time to spend with you."

"Maybe." Hugh rolled his eyes. "I'm not changing any diapers."

Dallas stared down at him. "I'm not talking about diapers. I'm talking about the time-honored tradition of big brotherhood." He pretended to size up the boy. "I don't know if you're ready for it... you're kinda short and," he held up the little boy's arm, "puny, so I don't think you can do it."

Talk about lighting a fire under the kid. He pulled himself up to his full height of four feet. "I'm not small or puny. I can be a big brother better than anyone."

"Okay, I believe you, but you've got to be willing to take on some pretty scary things. Big brotherhood is a secret club, and we only take men of good moral character."

"What's moral character?" Hugh stared solemnly up at his uncle. "Do I got it?"

"Well now, let me see." Dallas stopped and held the kid out in front of him. He made a big show of inspecting Hugh. "Yes, I do see some good moral character in you. Good moral character means being kind and honest and treating people fairly. Think you can do that?"

"I guess." Hugh didn't sound so sure. "What does that have to do with AG?"

Hugh was a smart one. Nothing got past him.

"You have to help take care of her. Rock her when she cries, play with her when she wants to play, and here's the most important part of big brotherhood, you have to protect her. Big brothers have to protect their little sisters and brothers. It's in the big brothers' code. Whether it's monsters under the bed or thunderstorms, you've got to be right there beside her to battle those monsters and then to hold her hand. She's a little tiny baby, so she's going to be scared, and you're going to have to protect her." Dallas looked down at him gravely. "Think you can do that?"

"I sure can. I'll protect her forever." Hugh nodded like he'd just been asked to protect the president of the United States.

"That's a good big brother." Dallas took the boy's hand and they walked toward the control room beside the quarry. "Now, tell me everything about your Aunt Rosie."

Now was as good a time as any to press the kid for info.

"Well, she's pretty and she makes really good birthday cake." According to Hugh, those were the only two qualities that mattered in his book. The kid was wise beyond his years.

"She is pretty. I don't know about the birthday cake, but I'm willing to keep an open mind." Dallas made sure to slow his pace to match Hugh's shorter legs. "Anything else?"

Hugh thought about it for a second. "My mom says that she's not a morning person—whatever that means."

"Not a morning person." He filed that bit of info away for future use. "What else?"

"She has a bunch of sisters, and when they're together they're really loud... kinda like when you get together with your brothers." Hugh shrugged his shoulders. "That's all I know... well, also, she smells good... like flowers."

Dallas had noticed that right off. She smelled like gardenias and lemons. He couldn't think of anything bad to say about gardenias or lemons. "Thanks for the info."

"No problem." Hugh shrugged a shoulder like it was no big deal. "Why are you asking about Aunt Rosie?"

Crap, that wise-beyond-his-years thing was turning on Dallas.

"No reason. Since she's moving here, I thought it would be nice if I got to know her better." That was reasonable and mostly true.

"Okay." Hugh looked up at Dallas. "Did you know that over a lifetime, the human body produces enough spit to fill two swimming pools?"

"I did not. Thanks for the tip." He hawked up a good-sized loogie. "I bet I can spit farther than you."

"No, you can't." Hugh hawked up his own.

They let them rip and Hugh was the clear winner.

"That was amazing. You've got some real skills, H-man." Dallas rustled the kid's hair. "Impressive."

Hugh smiled with his whole body. "Thanks. I've been practicing."

"It shows." Dallas nodded. "Practice makes perfect."

Hugh pointed to the row of green about a hundred feet in front of him. "Are those watermelons?"

"Yep. If we're going to blow stuff up, we need stuff to blow up. I thought watermelons would be nice and messy. Blowing stuff up isn't any fun unless you make a giant mess." If there was one thing Dallas knew, it was how to make a huge mess.

Three hours later, the quarry looked like a war had broken out between the watermelons, the cantaloupes, and the honeydews. It looked like the watermelons had taken the heaviest casualties. Chunks of melon were everywhere.

"I wish we'd had some pumpkins to blow up, but they're not in season." One side of Worth's mouth curled up in a smile. "Now those are really fun because they're pretty much hollow inside and you can really pack in the explosives."

"See? There." Dallas pointed to his brother. "I knew you weren't always a tight-ass—um... stick-in-the-mud."

They were working on not cussing around H-man, but sometimes things just slipped out.

Worth shot him a yeah-right smile. "I have been known on occasion to blow stuff up just for fun."

Dallas put a hand over his heart and wiped fake tears with the other. "This is a very proud moment for me. Finally, my baby brother has removed the stick from his ass —um... posterior region. I'm almost speechless."

"Good God, don't half-ass—um, halfway do it. Go all in

and be speechless. You'd be doing the world a favor." Worth clapped his brother on the back.

"Do you see all of this hate?" Dallas glanced at Hugh. "I've devoted my life to making sure my rule-following brother occasionally has fun and doesn't miss out on life, and all I get for my trouble is attitude." He shook his head in resignation. "It's a thankless job, but I'll keep at it because that's what family does—they keep going even in the face of rudeness and hatred."

Worth stifled a yawn as he made a big show of checking his watch. "You almost finished?"

Dallas thought about it for a while. "Yep."

The control booth's door creaked open and Rosie stepped inside. "It looks like a bomb went off in the produce aisle." She smiled at Hugh.

"We were just using fireworks to blow up melons." Hugh was an excellent liar.

Dallas was pretty sure that was a bad thing.

"If you're going to do something, do it well." She pointed to the melon destruction. "Looks like you did a wonderful job."

Dallas opened his mouth to take some of the credit for the "wonderful job," but his tongue peanut-buttered to the roof of his mouth. The only thing that came out was drool.

Rosie's gaze landed on him, and he couldn't move a muscle. It was only a matter of time before drool flowed out and dripped on his chin.

Rosie's brows bunched together like she hadn't quite seen anything like him, and then she turned to Worth. "I wanted to talk about the fireworks for the B&B grand opening." She pointed to the safety window that gave them the view outside. "That is, if there are any fireworks left." She grinned, and Dallas's heart nearly stopped. True, she wasn't grinning at him, but he still got to see it. He'd never seen anything as lovely as Rosie Gomez.

"I've got a plan. I'll email you the file with the drawings and you can tell me what works and what doesn't." Worth was so calm, cool, and collected.

Dallas's armpits started to sweat profusely. He was afraid all that sweat was going to drip down his body and pool around him.

This wasn't going so well.

"Okay then." Her gaze fell on Dallas again, and she shook her head like she didn't know what she was supposed to do with him. She shot him a puzzled smile. "Is he okay?" She nodded at Dallas.

"Yes, he's fine. When he was little, Mom dropped him on his head a bunch of times. You'll get used to it. The drooling's new, though. I'm sure it will pass in a minute or two." Worth was all smiles and helpfulness. As soon as Rosie was out of earshot, Dallas was going to kill him.

"So many things make sense now." She smiled brightly at him. "I was a coach for the Special Olympics for almost eight years. I bet you'd like it."

Oh my God. She thought he rode the short bus to school. He couldn't make his mouth work to tell her the truth.

Worth nodded. "I'm not sure he's that special, but I'll keep it in mind."

Yep, Worth had to die. And it needed to hurt really bad.

She knelt in front of Hugh. "Hey, Big H, Bear told me to tell you that he's ready to play some serious Monopoly and that I'm to drop you off at the house ASAP."

Hugh looked up at Dallas. "Are we done here?"

Dallas managed to nod his head once, but he couldn't stop staring at Rosie and the drool just kept coming.

Rosie took a step back, like Dallas had gone from special to disturbed, and opened the door for Hugh. "Let's hit the road, buddy."

When they'd finally driven away, Dallas regained control over his body.

"That was the most pathetic thing I've ever seen. It was worse than that time you cried until Lexi Hearsley slept with you." Worth shook his head. "I didn't think you could beat the tears-for-sex routine, but here you are being way more pathetic than that."

It wasn't like Dallas could deny it. "I have no idea what to do."

He knew that he and Rosie would end up together, but so far, the actual plan to get to that destination wasn't coming together.

Worth put his arm around his brother. "I would offer you some brotherly advice, like you should be yourself around her, but we both know that would be a horrible mistake. A little bit of you goes a long way. It's better for everyone involved that you just stare at her and drool."

"What's that supposed to mean?" Did Worth have feelings for her too? If he did, there was only one way out. Dallas was back to killing his favorite brother. Sure, it would hurt initially, but over time he'd get over it.

"Stop looking at me like you're picking out just the right urn for my remains." Worth smacked him on the back of the head. "The only feelings I have for Rosie are of the brotherly variety. You need to step up your game."

Trouble was, Dallas didn't have game around Rosie.

5

Rosie wasn't sure what to think about Dallas. Last night, no one had mentioned that he had cognitive disabilities. Surely it would have come up.

"You like your uncle Dallas a lot. Right?" She wasn't exactly pumping the kid for info. They were just having a conversation in her old Range Rover on the way to the main house.

"Yes, he's so much fun." Hugh thumbed behind him in the direction of the quarry. "When he and Worth—that's his twin brother, in case you didn't know they were twins—anyway, when they get together, they are so funny."

She wasn't sure beating the daylights out of each other qualified as fun, but she didn't know for sure, since she didn't have brothers. "Okay, what else?"

"What else, what?" Hugh looked up at her with his huge aqua eyes.

"What else do you like about him?" She couldn't get the picture of that drool out of her head. "Is he nice?"

"Yep, he's a good guy. He always has SweeTarts and lets me have some. He likes computer games and board games.

Once, he let me drive Worth's new truck, but we agreed that Worth didn't need to know about that. Dallas runs the exotic-animal ranch. He lets me help him feed all the animals. They have zebras and camels and all sorts of animals. Did you know sloths only poop once a week?" Hugh bounced up and down in his seat with excitement. "They have hunting, but only for deer. There's this big fence around the exotic ranch so no one hunts there."

"That's good, I guess." She knew where the food she ate came from, but she wasn't sure how she felt about hunting. "What else?"

"He has a huge TV and we have movie nights. I get to eat all the popcorn I want. Popcorn was invented by the Native Americans." It seemed that Hugh loved Dallas for his junk food.

"What does your mom think about the all-you-can-eat popcorn?" Rosie had a feeling that Justus didn't know. Not that she was a food nazi, but she liked to make sure Hugh ate some vegetables. Was corn still considered a vegetable if it was popped?

"She doesn't ask and I don't tell her." He was all self-importance. "Dallas, Worth, and I have a man code. That means girls aren't allowed, and what we do during man time is our own business."

She nodded. "I can see how important the man code is to you. I won't ask any more questions."

It was good for Hugh to have positive male role models. Although, she wasn't sure Worth and Dallas were positive role models. They sounded like big kids. Then again, weren't most men really just big kids?

"Today Dallas told me I've got a big job... big brothers are very important." His self-importance doubled.

"What do you mean?" She loved talking to Hugh. He was the most charming kid she'd ever met.

"I've got to protect AG. Also, I gotta play with her and rock her when she cries." He made it sound like he'd gotten a special assignment from the CIA.

"That is very important." She hoped she sounded sufficiently impressed. So, Dallas knew how to inspire a nine-year-old to start taking care of his little sister? Now that was impressive.

"I gotta kill all the monsters under her bed and help her not be scared during a thunderstorm." He counted off on his fingers. "And, I gotta make sure she's safe all the time."

"That does sound like a tough job. I'm glad you're her big brother, because you're the best big brother ever." She couldn't help but smile at his grown-up resolve to carry out his duties no matter what.

"I know." His tone said, "A man's gotta do what a man's gotta do."

She delivered him to Bear for the Monopoly marathon and headed to the bed-and-breakfast.

She pulled up next to the first teepee. Pride made her smile. This wasn't a conventional B&B. Luxury teepees and rustic-only-on-the-outside cabins were scattered along a beautiful stretch of the Guadalupe River. The teepees all had Native American tribal names, while the cabins were named after the men who'd settled Texas.

A large air-conditioned meeting room with a full kitchen was situated behind the teepees and cabins so that everyone had access to it. It could double as a dining room or a conference room for corporate events. They'd named it the Lodge.

She shaded her eyes from the sun as she grabbed the sketchbook she used to make notes and walked to the

Lodge. The workers were installing the granite countertops today. She wanted to make sure everything ran smoothly. In her experience, things ran better when she watched every step of the process. It wasn't micromanaging so much as being hands-on.

After flipping to the kitchen page in her book, she propped it up on a sawhorse the workers had used to make the cabinets. She glanced around the room. The cabinets were exactly as she'd planned—dark, rich cherry that would complement the Sienna Beige granite she'd personally picked out from the slabs at the granite yard. The white subway-tile backsplash gave the kitchen a clean look without being sterile. There were spaces for the commercial-grade appliances, and the soft-pearl-gray walls were warm and homey. The entire right wall had been painted with chalkboard paint so that she could keep the guests abreast of any and all activities or points of interest they might like to visit.

She nodded to herself. It was coming together nicely.

Thunder crackled in the distance.

It appeared that Hugh would get to protect AG from thunderstorms sooner than he'd expected. She could imagine him with his foam sword standing over her. Thank goodness AG loved him or she'd be terrified.

Light rain patted against the metal roof as thunder rattled against the windows.

Wouldn't you know it, she needed to check on the Villa at the top of the hill overlooking the vineyard. If she didn't get going, all she'd get for her trouble was a muddy mess.

Thunder rumbled again. The storm was getting closer.

She picked up her sketch pad, flipped the cover closed, and stuffed it inside her suit jacket. She threw open the front door and dashed out into the rain. When she was little, her mother had told her to run between the raindrops. She remembered trying to do just that.

Rosie shook her head as she opened the Ranger Rover's door. That memory of her mother was so clear to her. It had been during one of her mother's manic episodes. Bipolar disorder was a roller-coaster ride of the highest highs and the lowest lows. Looking back on it, she couldn't decide what was worse, the manic episodes or the depression. The only thing worse than either had been her mother's drug use.

She slammed the door and started up the Rover. Having four-wheel drive was a blessing out here. She put it in four-wheel high and drove across the low-water crossing to the other bank of the Guadalupe. She pulled into the Villa's crushed-granite parking pad, shoved her sketch pad in her leather work tote, and braced herself for the soggy jog ahead.

Now she was willing to admit that leaving the landscape natural and only cutting a golf-cart-sized path to the Villa had been a very bad idea. Lucy and Justus had tried to talk her out of it, but Rosie had insisted that the Villa, a.k.a. the honeymoon suite, needed to be private. She'd gotten caught up in the romance of it all. Big mistake... huge. She threw her phone into her work tote, made sure her iPad was inside, and zipped up the bag. She threw open the door and shoved her umbrella in the space between the door and the doorframe and hit the button to open it. Three of the skinny metal bars that were supposed to hold it up failed, and one side of the umbrella was limp and completely useless. She'd forgotten to replace it after it had broken the last time she'd used it. She tossed the worthless thing in the backseat, held her leather bag over her head, and slid out of the Rover. Her feet and her favorite black Jimmy Choos hit a mud puddle and sank a good two inches. She pried her feet out of the mud and slogged up the winding limestone path up the hill to the Villa. What she wouldn't give for a golf cart, or even an umbrella that worked, or heck, some ugly work boots.

She rolled her eyes.

It was a sad state of affairs that she was even entertaining the idea of ugly work boots.

She trudged up the five steps onto the front patio and twisted the handle of the front door. It was locked.

"Really? Are you kidding me right now?" she screamed, in case anyone cared.

Everyone had told her that it wasn't necessary to lock the doors, but she'd insisted.

The storm was raging now. Sheets of rain pelted the aluminum roof. She steeled herself for another run in the rain to get the keys, and then the mental image of the Villa's keys sitting on the cottage's kitchen counter popped into her head.

For someone who was known for her planning skills, she really was knocking unprepared out of the park. She glanced down the hill in the direction of her Rover. She dropped her bag on one of the wicker rocking chairs on the front porch. Was it her imagination or did it sound like the water in the Guadalupe River was getting closer?

The low-water crossing would be completely covered by a raging froth of white-water rapids by now. It didn't look like she was going anywhere, because even the best four-wheel drive in the world could make it across the river.

"Turn around, don't drown" was a popular battle cry in Central Texas, particularly in what was known as Flash Flood Alley.

She shivered. The 2015 Wimberley, Texas, flood had taken the lives of twelve people.

She rolled her eyes. The Texas Rose Ranch was nowhere near Wimberley.

Still the rain beat down and the river waters rose. Rosie knew that it wasn't necessarily the rain right here that caused the rise in the river. It was the rain upstream barreling downriver that did the most damage. She sat in one of the wicker rockers and pulled her cell out of her bag. Just to be on the safe side, she'd text CanDee, Lucy, and Justus that she was at the Villa.

She unlocked her phone and typed in the text and hit send. The angry-red "not delivered" message appeared under the text. She looked in the upper-left-hand corner of the screen, and sure enough, "no service" glared back at her. The best thing about the Villa, apart from the fantastic view and plush interior, was that it came with high-speed internet. Unfortunately, the satellite internet and TV weren't scheduled to be installed until next week.

She slapped her phone down on the black antique wrought-iron table between the rocking chairs. There was no way around it, she was stuck out here until the water receded. On a long sigh, she pulled out her iPad and hit the Safari icon. Nothing happened. Duh, no internet.

Holy hell, she was stuck in the middle of nowhere, with work to do and absolutely no way to do it. She shucked off her soaked-through suit jacket and hung it on the back of her chair. Her white blouse now had see-through blotches, but it wasn't like she could take that off and hang it up to dry. She slid off her shoes and leaned back in the rocking chair and checked her watch. She rocked back and forth several times and checked her watch again.

How was it that only sixteen seconds had passed?

What had people done before the internet?

This was like being stuck in the 1800s. All she needed

was a hoopskirt and a mint julep to sip while she rocked on the front porch.

Her foot wiggled with the need to do something.

She checked her watch. Only four more seconds had ticked by.

If only she had her laptop. At least she could catch up on some paperwork. Wait, hold on. She had her phone and her iPad. She picked up her iPad and tried to pull up her to-do list. Dang it, she kept everything in the cloud.

She deserved an overly dramatic smack on the forehead.

This was her own personal hell.

Her mother had always said that idle hands do the devil's work. If only. Her idle hands couldn't do any work.

The wind kicked up and the rain came faster. She hugged herself, fighting off the chill. This morning it had been a humid eighty-five degrees. Now it felt like a cold front had knocked down those numbers by at least ten to fifteen degrees.

She was wet, stranded, and bored. It was going to be a long afternoon.

6

Dallas sat with his feet propped up against the wooden rail of his front porch. Underneath him, the old kitchen chair creaked as he leaned it back on two legs. He liked the rain. There was something peaceful about sitting outside and watching the rain.

He grabbed the bottle of Shiner at his feet and sipped long and deep. The pitter-pat of raindrops on the metal roof of his two-story house was calming. Unfortunately, it was also conducive to self-reflection, and man, did he ever not need that right now.

He was willing to admit that today with Rosie hadn't gone well. In fact, it might be the all-time lowest of the low points in their relationship. How much worse could it get?

Short of running her over with his truck or accidentally shooting her with his hunting rifle, what could be worse than having her think he was a drooling weirdo?

He couldn't think of a thing.

As long as he kept his truck and his rifle away from her, there was nowhere to go but up.

Come to think of it, did they even really have a relationship?

The rain picked up, and lightning stabbed across the horizon. It was only six, but the angry gray clouds were so thick, it was almost full dark.

Rosie Posy had walked into his life and turned it upside down. Not that he minded, but he sure would like to get to the part where they lived happily ever after. He could see their life together so clearly. Because she wasn't a morning person, he'd get up and make breakfast so whenever she rolled out of bed it would be waiting for her. On second thought, he'd make breakfast and put it in the fridge before getting back in bed with her and waking her up properly.

He liked that version better.

When it came to Rosie, he had lots of fantasies—most of them involved her minus those tailored business suits she favored. He couldn't help but smile. Yep, he'd love nothing more than peeling her out of that all-business navy-blue suit that matched her eyes she'd been wearing this morning.

Worth's truck came splashing up the driveway.

Dallas took a deep breath and let it out slowly. He really wasn't in the mood for company. He just wanted to sit on his porch, drink his beer, and watch the rain.

Worth rolled down the window and yelled something, but the storm was too loud. Like hell was Dallas walking out to Worth's truck. What could possibly be so important that his brother had braved the storm?

Worth jumped out of the driver's seat, slammed the door, and ran to the porch. "Why in the hell don't you answer your damn phone?"

"What?" Dallas looked around for his phone, and not finding it, he felt around for it in his back pockets. It wasn't there either. "I must have left it inside. What's wrong?"

Worth was a lot of things, but alarmist wasn't one of them.

Fear prickled the hairs at the back of Dallas's neck. Something was wrong.

"Rosie's missing. According to Hugh, she went to check on the cabins." Worth pointed to his truck. "We need to find her, now."

Dallas was on his feet as soon as he heard the word Rosie. He ran down the steps, barely registering the rain as he slipped behind the wheel. "I'll drive."

For once, Worth didn't argue. He opened the passenger's-side door and got in. "We checked the cabins, but... um..."

"What?" Dallas's heart was beating so hard it was a wonder he didn't have a stroke. Dallas had a bad feeling. Worth knew something he didn't want to tell Dallas. "What!"

"It may be nothing... but one of the hands saw her Rover washing downstream." Worth cleared his throat. "She wasn't in it. It was upside down."

Oh God. Oh Jesus. No. The last time the Guadalupe River had flooded, it had swept a dozen people downstream, killing nine of them. Rosie couldn't be dead, she just wasn't. He loved her and he hadn't even told her.

He stomped on the gas, and the truck's back tires spun before catching traction. He floored it in the direction of the cabins. "Did you check the cabins and teepees? Maybe she's in one them waiting out the storm."

Please God, let her be okay.

"Yes, we've checked every single building on this side of the river and we can't find her—" His brother's voice cracked. "Anywhere."

"What about the Villa or the fire lookout?" They hadn't

checked everywhere. Rosie was smart and levelheaded. She was safe... she was safe... she was safe. Surely, if he repeated it a million times, it would make it true.

"I'm sure she's fine." Worth was going for soothing, but his voice was too frightened to pull it off. "She's probably all warm and cozy next to a fire drinking a steaming mug of hot chocolate and waiting out the storm."

"Yeah, uh huh." Dallas knew Worth was doing his best to assure him that Rosie was okay, but he was making it worse.

"We'll find her and all have a big laugh about it." Worth's voice shook with concern.

The world would be a much better place if his brother spontaneously went mute.

Dallas pulled onto the old two-track road that led down to the river. He parked next to his mother's black Tahoe. Several trucks were clumped together, while everyone stood under the Lodge's covered patio, huddled around some sort of map.

Why were they just standing around? Why weren't they out looking for Rosie?

He jumped out of the truck and ran over to the Lodge. Everyone but Rosie was there—his mother and father, his brothers Cinco and Rowdy, Lefty, plus he counted ten other ranch hands all looking up at him.

His mother went over to him and put her arm around him. "She's probably safe and waiting out the storm some-where." She tried to sound convincing, but it fell short. "I'm sure she's fine." It sounded like she was trying to make herself believe it.

"Where is her Rover?" Dallas needed to be all business now. He pushed all worry aside and went into crisis-handling mode.

Tiny, who was in fact the largest man Dallas had ever

seen, raised his hand. "I saw it float by Lehman's Gap a little over an hour ago."

"Some other of them boys," Lefty nodded to the ranch hands, "saw it pass by the bunkhouses a little bit after that. Son, just because they seen her car don't mean she was in it."

Lefty had been Dallas's grandfather's best friend, and after Grandpa Rose had died, Lefty had stepped in to fill the hole.

"Have all of the cabins been checked?" Dallas finger combed his hair. He had no idea what to do now.

"Yes." His father put his hand on Dallas's shoulder. "We've checked and double-checked and triple-checked."

Dallas scanned the faces surrounding him. "Where's Hugh?"

"He's with Justus and CanDee and AG. They're all at the cottage in case Rosie comes home." Cinco nodded in the general direction of the cottage.

"Okay, that's good. What did Hugh say exactly?" He needed to know everything.

"That she was headed to the teepees and cabins to check on them." His father pulled him in for a hug.

"Besides the buildings, what has been checked? Has anyone walked up and down the riverbank? She might be hurt." He didn't want to think of her as hurt... or worse.

"We have men out doing that now." His mother laced her fingers through his father's. "Even if the rain lets up now, according to the National Weather Service and the Guadalupe-Blanco River Authority, the water might not crest until day after tomorrow. They've had so much rain upstream." His mother sounded hopeless, and she never sounded hopeless.

"The water is higher than it's ever been. That includes

the 1998 flood." His father left out the part that the 1998 flood had hit the hundred-year floodplain and was the worst flood recorded in Central Texas history.

"We have to do something. We can't just stand around doing nothing." All he needed was a flashlight, and he'd go find her himself. As soon as he found Rosie, he was buying her a satellite phone and supergluing it to her left hand. That way she'd always be in touch. "What about a helicopter and life flight or something? Doesn't the coast guard have some sort of helicopter for things like this?"

He was grasping at straws, but they were all he had to hold onto.

"They're triaging the calls." His mother looked him square in the eye. "They aren't taking on any search and rescue, only airlifting those that have been identified as needing help."

Translation, they were only airlifting people they knew were alive, and not searching for those who were missing.

Why in the hell didn't the Texas Rose Ranch have a helicopter? If he bought one, how fast could he have it delivered? He could rent a helicopter. There had to be one around here somewhere that he could rent.

"I think we need to face the facts..." His father pulled him in for another hug. "She was either swept away or she's on the other side of the river." Judging by his father's tone, he thought it was door number one.

"Fine, it sounds like you have this side of the river covered. How do I get to the other side?" He wasn't stopping until he found her. "There has to be a way across the river."

He could drive to Roseville and cross the bridge, only there were three low-water crossings on the way. He turned to Cinco. "Didn't one of our ancestors cross the river in a flood in 1900?"

"Are you talking about Dutch Gering during the flood of 1913?" Cinco's eyes squinted up as he shook his head. "He died, and that's why we call the place he tried to cross Gering Ford."

Dallas snapped his fingers and pointed to Cinco. "Great idea. Gering Ford. It's upstream a bit so the water's probably shallower, plus it's a ford, which is nature's low-water crossing."

As long as he had a plan, he wouldn't think the worse. Every second they wasted, the river rose even higher.

"Son, you can't cross Gering Ford. The water's rushing too fast." His father was always the voice of reason. "There isn't a truck in the world that wouldn't stall out, and that's assuming the current didn't take you."

Worth stepped up. "What about on horseback?"

Everyone looked at Cinco, who spent a lot of time in the saddle and oversaw the horses.

He shook his head. "The current is too fast even for Back Strap."

Back Strap was a Clydesdale.

"Am I correct in assuming that you're going to do this no matter what we say?" His mother crossed her arms and managed to look down her nose at him, even though she was a good foot shorter than he was.

She knew him too well.

"Yes." His family didn't seem to have the sense of urgency he did.

"Since you're likely going to kill yourself to get to her, we have to help you no matter how stupid the plan." His mother huffed out a frustrated breath. "The zip line."

"What zip line?" They didn't have a zip line. When had they gotten a zip line?

His mother rolled her eyes. "The one you and Worth

made in high school out of some old cabling and U-bolts so you could get your cases of beer to the other side of the river and stow them in the old icehouse."

How had she known about that?

She shot him an I'm-all-knowing look.

"Think it will hold me?" Dallas chewed on his bottom lip, waiting for confirmation. It was a shot. Granted, it was terrible, but it was something.

"Yes, CanDee and I tried it last week, on the off chance it still worked and we could call it an amenity for our guests." His mother was so matter-of-fact.

"Let me get this straight, you risked your life on some old piece of crap our son built over a decade ago?" His father looked pissed. The man rarely lost his temper, but when he did, it was good and lost. His father pointed to his mother. "We're going to revisit this, but right now, do you think that zip line is strong enough to hold Dallas and withstand the wind and rain?"

"Yes, we played on it for several hours and it seemed sturdy." Dallas's mother seemed to wither a bit as his father glared at her.

"Just for the sake of argument, let's say you do make it to the other side of the river. You still have at least a half-mile slog to the Villa through zero visibility. I was the Eagle Scout, remember?" Worth thumbed his chest. "You couldn't use a compass if your life depended on it." He paused for dramatic effect. "And it will depend on it."

"He's right." Cinco stepped to Worth's right. "Right now, we don't know that Rosie is in danger, so going off half-cocked and putting yourself into real danger doesn't make sense."

"What if it were CanDee?" Dallas didn't have time to argue his case. He needed to get to the zip line. He felt around in his pockets. Where had he put Worth's keys? Were they still in the truck?

"If it were CanDee, I'd already be on that zip line." Cinco reached around Lefty and picked up a backpack. "Justus and CanDee packed this just in case. There are a couple of flashlights and extra batteries. Justus knew you might go looking for Rosie at the Villa, so she packed some supplies for the two of you."

Dallas grabbed the backpack and was in the truck before he had time to think about it.

"I'll drive." Worth practically threw him out of the way and slid behind the wheel.

Everyone else ran out to their respective vehicles.

Dallas died a thousand times in the five minutes it took to get to the zip line. The water lapped at the cypress tree with the metal cable wrapped around it. It was pitch black outside, and the wind howled like a banshee. Worth backed his truck up to the cypress.

Dallas was out of the truck and climbing into the bed so he could climb up to the zip line. By feeling around, he located the rickety wooden platform. A flashlight beam hit the platform, lighting it up. Other flashlight beams lit up the tree. His family was lighting the way.

He shrugged on the backpack, felt around for the wooden seat they'd used for the beer, and climbed onto it. It creaked under his weight, but it held.

"Once you're on the other side, grab a flashlight and wave the beam up in the air so we know you're safe. Then get to the highest ground possible and stay to the left. The icehouse is about halfway to the Villa." Worth touched Dallas's shoulder. "If you die, I'm going to be so pissed."

"I'd hate to piss you off." Dallas took a deep breath, reached over his head, and released the clamp.

As he flew through the air, the wind stabbed at him and rain sharper than shards of broken glass tore at his skin. A huge gust of wind nearly knocked him off the seat, but he righted himself at the last moment and managed to stay seated. The cable jangled back and forth, slowing his progress. He got halfway over the river and stopped. He couldn't see a thing, so he got his legs under him and knelt on the seat. He felt around. Tree leaves were caught in the trolley mechanism. He pulled a handful out and swung his body weight back and then forward, trying to gain some momentum. The seat didn't move. He was stuck.

With no other option, he reached up with both hands, curled one leg around the cable and then the other. He inched his way across the river, battling the fierce wind shaking the cable. About five feet from the shore, he felt the cable give way, and he hung on for all he was worth. The cable ripped in half, and he took a nosedive into the water.

Cold water rushed at him from all sides, but he held on tight. He wheezed in gulps of air as the backpack pulled him down. He couldn't shrug out of it because then he'd have to let go of the line. Water sucked him down, so he kicked his booted feet like his life depended on it.

Inch by inch, he pulled himself to the bank and crawled out of the water. He threw off the backpack, pulled out a zip-top plastic bag, and grabbed a dry flashlight. Whoever'd had the presence of mind to wrap everything in watertight bags had just moved up to the top of his Christmas list.

He flicked on the flashlight and waved it back and forth. The beam of light barely broke through the cutting rain. He hoped they could see it on the other side of the river.

He closed the pack and stuffed his arms through the straps. He rolled onto his knees and used a nearby tree to stand. White-hot pain shot up from his left ankle. He doubled over, but quickly righted himself. He had a half-mile trek through a watery hell, his ankle be damned.

Rain slashed at Dallas's face as he limped to higher ground. The flashlight beam only cut through a foot of the path in front of him. The wind howled like a commercial plane taking off as it did its best to knock him over. His left ankle was sprained, or maybe even broken, and every step sent a bolt of pain up his leg, but he'd made it this far and he wasn't about to give up.

Rosie Posy, I'm coming for you.

7

There was something peaceful and primal about a good old-fashioned thunderstorm. Rosie stood at the stove stirring a pot of canned chicken noodle soup that she'd found in the pantry.

The built-in microwave had yet to be installed, so she was cooking like they did in the 1950s.

It had been Lucy's idea to stock some nonperishables in the Villa in case the guests preferred days upon days of privacy instead of going out for food. The diesel-powered whole-house generator had been a necessity because this side of the river didn't have electricity. All Rosie had to do was flick the light switch and voilà—lights.

Lightning arched across the sky to the west so often that the effect was like a strobe light. Thunder rattled the lead-glass windows. It sounded like thunder and lightning were battling to the death, while she was all warm and cozy inside.

She glanced at the small broken windowpane on the patio door. She'd had to do it. The only other choice was to spend the night on the front porch. She could probably find someone to fix it tomorrow or the next day. Convincing repairmen to come all the way out to the ranch was proving to be difficult. On second thought, she bet Lefty could fix it. It seemed like he could fix just about anything.

Thunder shook the front door.

It was odd, she could swear she heard someone yelling. It had to be the wind. No one would be fool enough to be out in this storm.

Overhead, the thunder stopped rolling, but the front door still pounded.

She ran to the front door and turned on the porch light.

Was it her imagination or was Dallas Rose leaning against the front door?

She unlocked it and pulled it open.

"You're okay." He was soaked to the bone. "Thank God, you're okay."

His eyes drank her in, and then they rolled back in his head and he swayed.

Rosie caught him before he crumbled to the floor. "Let's get you to the sofa."

"I had to find you and make sure you were okay." Dallas was a heap of deadweight. "We need to let everyone know you're okay."

"I wish we could, but I don't have cell coverage out here." She shouldered his weight and practically dragged him to the sofa. "How did you get here?"

Surely he hadn't swum across the river. With the rising floodwater, it would have been extremely dangerous. Guilt pricked her heart. It sounded like the whole family was worried about her.

"Zip line." He said it as if it were the most sensible thing in the world. He pushed at her hands. "I can walk."

She let go and then caught him before he melted to the floor. "Humor me and let me help you."

He shivered.

"You're freezing. Let's get you into a hot bath. I have some canned chicken noodle soup on the stove." She could always warm up another can. He needed the soup more than she did.

"No, no, I'm fine. Don't go to any trouble." He tried to stand on his own, and she saw him press his lips together, as if to stifle a scream.

"Are you hurt?" She didn't see any blood. Then again, his clothes were covered in muck and plastered to his body, so it was hard to tell much of anything.

"My left ankle. I think it's broken." His voice was controlled, like he was doing everything he could to keep from screaming.

She shuffled him into the bathroom, propped him up against the vanity, put the stopper into the claw-foot tub drain, and twisted the knobs for hot and then cold water. Without thinking, she picked up the plastic bottle of bubble bath and poured in a generous amount. He probably wasn't a bubbles man, but it was too late now.

"Let's get you out of those wet clothes." She turned back toward him, not sure if she should help him undress. Could he undress himself?

Awkwardly, he shuffled the backpack off his shoulder and handed it to her. "There's a satellite phone in here. Can you let everyone know we're okay? You have to use it outside with a clear line of sight to the sky." He took in her rumpled navy suit that she was sure had splotches of mud from helping him to the bathroom. "Sorry you have to go outside."

She waved it off. "Do you need help with your clothes?"

He looked like he needed a trip to the emergency room.

"I'll be fine. Go make the call and let everyone know I made it here and that you're okay." He was particularly articulate today. No intellectual challenges at all.

She took the backpack from him and turned to the door, but he put a hand on her shoulder.

"One more thing." His eyes searched her face.

"Yes?" She'd never noticed the gold flecks in his aqua-blue eyes.

He leaned down and kissed her. His lips were soft at first and then demanding. His tongue parted her lips and she returned the kiss. Heat bloomed in her core and radiated out. The chemical reaction of attraction snaked through her body. She wanted Dallas... she wanted him very much.

He leaned back against the granite vanity and pulled her with him. His lips left hers as he trailed kisses down her neck. He shuffled his weight and his whole body went rigid, like he was in pain. He broke contact and sucked in a breath between gritted teeth.

She stepped back. "You kissed me and I liked it." She could feel her face turning a nice shade of apple red. "I said that out loud, didn't I?"

"Yep." He grinned. "You sure did."

Oh God, mortified wasn't a strong enough word for what she felt right now.

"I'm gonna just... you know." She pointed to the backpack. "You're fine, I mean... will be fine taking off your clothes... or I could help you. I'm happy to help you strip down." She shook her head trying to make some coherent words come out. "I didn't mean... well... I kind of meant it. I'm going. Peace out." She threw up a peace sign. "I don't why I just did that."

She managed to stumble out the door and close it

behind her. In all of recorded time, she didn't think there had ever been a more embarrassing moment. Perhaps she was being a little overly dramatic, but still. Had she really said, "Peace out"?

Opening the backpack, she riffled around until she found the satellite phone.

She opened the front door and stepped out onto the porch. She turned on the sat phone. It looked like it was working without having to leave the porch. Was using it just like using a cell phone? From her left jacket pocket, she pulled out her cell, looked up Lucy's number, and dialed. It rang and rang and rang.

The phone connected. "This is Dr. Lucy Rose. I'm not able to take your call right now, but please leave me a message. I'll call you back as soon as I'm able. Have a wonderful day."

After the beep, Rosie said, "Lucy, I just wanted to let you know that Dallas made it to the Villa. I think his ankle is broken, but I don't know for sure. We're both here and we'll wait out the storm. Thanks." She hit end.

Lucy probably didn't have cell service. She looked up the main house's phone number and dialed it.

"Rose residence." It was Mary, the housekeeper.

"Hi, Mary, this is Rosie. Can you please tell Dr. and Mr. Rose that I'm okay and that Dallas made it to the Villa? I think his left ankle is broken, but I'm not sure..."

"Just a moment, here she is." Mary was always efficient.

"Rosie?" Lucy sounded tired. "Is Dallas there? Are you both okay?"

"Yes, we're both at the Villa. I think he broke his ankle, but I'm not sure." She had no idea what to do for a broken ankle besides ice it.

"You need to immobilize and ice it. Do you have any ibuprofen?" Lucy was in doctor mode.

"Yes, I have some in my work bag. How much should I give him?" Should she be taking notes?

"Is it bleeding, or is the bone sticking out?" Lucy's tone was flat, like she was in the ER calling out orders for her staff to follow.

"I don't know. He was wearing cowboy boots. I'm outside and he's inside taking a bath. Want me to go check?" Should she hang up, go check on Dallas, and call Lucy back?

"No, if he walked there, the chances are good that he doesn't have an open fracture. After we hang up, you can check on him and call me back if the bone is sticking out. Right now, give him eight hundred milligrams of ibuprofen now and two hundred every two hours. Make sure he takes it with food or a glass of milk. The ibuprofen will take the edge off the pain and keep the swelling down. Also, you need to apply some sort of compression wrapping. Use the RICE method. Rest, ice, compress, and elevate." Lucy took a deep breath. "It might be a couple of days before we can get you out of there. I know Dallas is in pain, but his injury isn't life-threatening. All of the available emergency personnel and helicopters are in search-and-rescue mode. Since neither one of you are in immediate danger, I hate to tell you this, but you're not a priority."

"We're fine. We have food, electricity, and we're safe. I promise I'll take good care of Dallas." At least taking care of him was something to do. She'd never not been able to work. Two days with no way to get work done. It was a waste of perfectly good time.

"Just so you know, he about lost it when he found out you were missing. I was afraid he'd try to swim across the river to get to you. Nothing or no one could have stopped him from making sure you were okay. He's got one big crush on you." Lucy's tone was back to worried mom.

"He has a crush on me? That explains the kiss." She touched her bottom lip at the memory.

"He kissed you?" Some of the worry in Lucy's voice dissipated. "Please, tread lightly. Occasionally he irritates me, but I love him."

"I'll do my best." Rosie had never intentionally hurt anyone—well, except for the vendors who didn't make good on their promises to her. To be fair, she hadn't hurt them so much as made their lives a living hell until they delivered.

"I know you will, but he's still my baby." Lucy was all tired concern. There was some shuffling on her end. "I have to go. Bear's dying to yell at me for playing on the zip line the other day. Call back if you need anything. I'll have the house phone with me at all times. Otherwise, call us first thing in the morning."

"Okay. Thank everyone for me. Dallas said y'all were out looking for me." She hated that she'd worried them.

"I will." Lucy stifled a yawn. "I'm so glad you're both safe."

Lucy hung up.

All of this fuss over her. Usually, Rosie went out of her way to be as low maintenance as possible. She wasn't being ungrateful, but it seemed like overkill. Couldn't they see her Rover from the other side of the river? She glanced in the general direction of the path where her Rover was parked. Since the Villa was on the top of the hill overlooking the Texas Hill Country, she couldn't see her car. With the storm, she couldn't see ten feet in front of her, so maybe they couldn't either?

She turned off the phone to preserve the battery and headed back inside.

After a brief internal debate, she settled on knocking on the bathroom door instead of just opening it. The water wasn't running, so he was probably in the tub. She did her best to not picture him naked.

Wow, could he ever kiss. She felt it all the way down to her toes.

Using her right index finger, she knocked lightly on the door. "Are you okay? I spoke to your mother and told her that you made it here and that we're both safe. I told her about your ankle. She wanted to know if it's bleeding or if the bone is sticking out through the skin."

"I don't know." He sounded exhausted. "It's fine, you can come in."

Tentatively, she opened the door and poked her head in. She kept her eyes on the floor in case he was lounging in the tub.

"I can't get my boots off." He sounded more than a little frustrated with himself.

She walked into the bathroom. "Let me help."

He was shirtless, sprawled out on the floor, with his jeans pulled down to his knees. She tried not to notice that he was a boxer-brief kinda man. Also, she tried to keep her eyes from licking the peaks and valleys of his washboard abs, but they kept straying off the floor where she tried to make them count the crisp white subway tiles.

"I don't own cowboy boots, but I'm pretty sure you're supposed to take them off before your pants." She knelt in front of him.

"Everyone's a critic." A muscle twitched in his jaw, and she realized that he was biting his bottom lip in an effort to hold back the pain.

She tugged at the heel of his right boot and slipped it off, uncovering a white tube sock. Her eyes trained on his face. "Ready for the other one?"

His eyes met hers, and one corner of his mouth turned up in a grin. "As ready as I'll ever be."

With one hand, she grabbed the heel and positioned her other hand on top of the boot. "On three. One." She whipped off the boot in one single motion.

"Damn," he screamed at the top of his lungs. "What happened to three?"

"Element of surprise. One of my sisters used to be a medical assistant for a pediatrician. She always kept the syringe for the vaccinations behind her back and stabbed the kids in the arm before they had time to think about it. The poor kids always looked a little confused, like they knew they should cry, but the almost-painless shot really took the wind out of their sails." She grinned. "Element of surprise. Now I have to take off your sock. This time I promise to go on three."

She slid her hand up his pant leg and grabbed the top of the sock. "On three. One." She ripped the sock off.

"You did it again. What happened to you promising to wait until three?" He looked a lot like those kids after the surprise vaccination.

"I lied and you still fell for it. Element of surprise. Works every time." She slipped his other sock off and then pulled his jeans down over his right leg. "Guess what?"

"You're going to tell me to count to three and then you're going to pull my jeans off on one?" He couldn't be in too much pain, because he was grinning.

"Yep, you guessed it." She rolled the jeans up so she could get them off of him in one quick tug. "On three. One, two." She ripped them off.

"Somehow I knew that was going to happen, and yet I

still wasn't ready for it." He shook his head. "What does that say about me?"

"You're far too trusting." She glanced at his left ankle. Splotches of purple dotted the skin and it was swollen to twice the size of his right. There was an odd hump on the side. She had practically no medical training, but even she could tell there was something wrong with it.

She pointed to the boxer-briefs and did her best to keep her eyes on his face. "Are you ready to remove those?"

"I'm going to defy convention and leave them on for now." With his left leg out straight, he heaved himself up and then not-so-gracefully lowered himself into the bubble bath. "What made you think I'm a bubble-bath kinda man?"

"I didn't. I like bubble baths, so reaching for the bubbles was more of a habit." She grabbed a towel and placed it on the tray next to the tub. She picked up his clothes and wadded them into a ball. "I'll put these on to wash." She headed out of the room, stopped at the doorway, and turned back to him. "I'm bringing you some hot chicken noodle soup and a whole bunch of ibuprofen—doctor's orders.

He wiggled around in the tub, came up with his boxers, wrung them out, and tossed them onto the pile of clothes in her arms. "If you're going to wash my clothes anyway, I'd appreciate if you'd add those."

"No problem." She did her level best to not think about him being naked in all of that hot, bubbly heaven.

She closed the door behind her and sucked on her bottom lip. If any more sexual attraction swirled between them, she'd be shucking off her clothes and joining him.

She'd never been one for one-night stands, but she was seriously considering taking casual sex up as a hobby. It beat the hell out of tennis.

If that kiss was any indication, Dallas would be mind-blowing between the sheets. She cradled the wet clothes tighter and told herself that mixing business and pleasure was a bad idea. Hell, she rarely mixed pleasure with pleasure.

He was hot, naked, and just on the other side of the door.

It seemed that the storm raging outside wasn't the most dangerous thing she'd be dealing with tonight.

8

D allas relaxed back against the tub and sank lower into the bubbles. It had been one hell of a night. The storm and the death-defying zip-line ride didn't come close to the adrenaline rush of kissing Rosie.

He'd finally done it, and damn if she hadn't kissed him right back. But his most favorite part was watching the dazed expression on her face and turning the tables on her. For once, he was the coherent one.

He laced his fingers behind his head and tried not to look at his ankle. He was almost sure it was broken.

Truth was, right now it didn't hurt all that much, as long as he didn't put any pressure on it. Maybe it was the sexual endorphins flooding his brain with all sorts of feel-good chemicals or just finally getting a taste of Rosie, but he'd have to give this night a big ole thumbs-up. It might rank up there in the top five best nights of his life.

There was a soft knock at the bathroom door.

"Come in." He could barely contain the giddy vibe coursing through his body. It was stupid to be this happy about kissing someone, but it wasn't like he could change how he felt.

Rosie walked in carrying a tray. The tray held a bowl with steam wafting off of it, the chemical ice pack from the large first-aid kit his mother had set up herself, a white plastic bottle of pills, and a bottle of water. There was also a half-used roll of silver duct tape.

What in the hell was that for?

And where had she gotten a serving tray? He hadn't thought the Villa would be stocked with kitchenware yet, but apparently Rosie had thought of everything.

She nudged the vanity stool out from under the counter with her foot and pushed it over next to the tub. She set the tray on the stool.

"Isn't that your dinner?" Like hell was he taking food meant for her. He'd sooner starve to death.

"It's fine. I've got another can warming on the stove. You need to eat this before," she waggled the pill bottle, "I give you these. Your mother's orders."

As long as she was going to eat too. He leaned over, picked up the spoon, and scooped up a healthy bit of Campbell's chicken noodle.

"Your ankle looks bad." She picked up the duct tape and unwrapped a long piece.

He eyed the duct tape. "You got me, what are you planning on doing with that?"

He wasn't normally into bondage, but he liked to think of himself as open-minded.

She unrolled even more. "I have to wrap your ankle. I don't have an ACE bandage, but I always carry duct tape with me."

He eyed his hairy ankle. "I don't think so."

"Scared of a little duct tape?" She arched an eyebrow. "Man up."

"The application of the duct tape doesn't bother me. It's the removal that I'd rather not have to endure." His mother hadn't raised a fool.

She bent over his ankle, judging the best way to wrap it. Her shirt fell open, and he could see quite a lot of cleavage and one killer low-cut white-lace bra.

"On second thought, I probably should have my ankle wrapped." Cleavage was cleavage, and hers was of special interest for him. Did she always wear fancy underwear? Were her panties as lacy? He could stand to find out firsthand.

With all of the concentration of a nuclear physicist splitting an atom, she began the process of wrapping his ankle.

"Why do you always carry duct tape?" He wasn't trying to stall her so her shirt would hang open longer, he was merely making polite conversation.

"You can use it for anything. I've planned lots of weddings. Things always happen. Rip the hem in your dress and tape it up. Need to fix a plunging neckline that plunges a little too much, use duct tape. If the bumper falls off of the groom's car because his best man tied a full-grown javelina to it, just cut the javelina free and duct-tape the bumper back on." She bent even lower, used her teeth to cut the duct tape, and gently patted the end down.

"Javelinas, now there's a species that deserves to be hunted into extinction." He could see her taking on a pissed-as-hell javelina. His money was on Rosie. "That last one didn't really happen."

"I couldn't have made that up if I tried." She went to the linen closet and grabbed a small fluffy towel. She wrapped it around the ice pack and gently placed the whole thing around his ankle. "Does that hurt?"

"Only when I move it." He spooned in another mouthful of soup. "What's the worst thing that's happened at one of your weddings?" He wasn't chatting her up so much as trying to spend more time with her. He had a feeling that if she didn't have something else to do, she'd quickly leave the bathroom.

She leaned against the vanity and tried to look nonchalant, but she was failing miserably. She folded her arms and then unfolded them and then went back to folding them. "Besides the bride and/or groom not showing up, which, by the way, happens about fifteen percent of the time, the worst thing to happen was the wedding party almost drowning." When she talked about her work, her navy-blue eyes sparkled.

"Come on, don't leave me hanging. What happened?" She was smart and beautiful and funny. It was probably too early to ask her to marry him.

"Actually, it's happened twice. The first almost drowning was a minister who performed the wedding. The couple had met while scuba diving in Cozumel. It turned out that they lived two blocks from each other in downtown Austin. So, anyway, they wanted a scuba diving wedding. We were in the middle of planning a destination wedding in Cozumel when the groom's mother had a heart attack and couldn't travel to Cozumel. The bride and groom decided to tie the knot at Windy Point on Lake Travis." From the linen closet, she picked up a washcloth and used it to wipe down the vanity.

He was coming to find out that she wasn't one to sit still. "That doesn't sound dangerous." He didn't know much about Windy Point or Lake Travis, but it all sounded normal.

"I guess I forgot to mention that they wanted to get married underwater." She opened the cabinet under the sink, pulled out a bottle of glass cleaner, and sprayed the mirror. "The entire wedding party—minus the groom's mother—and all of the guests were to meet underwater for the ceremony." She wiped the mirror with the washcloth and then wiped down the doorframe. "Have you ever been scuba diving?"

"No, have you?" There was so much he didn't know about her.

"Yes, I go a couple of times a year." She stowed the glass cleaner back under the sink.

He couldn't quite picture her scuba diving, but he could imagine her in a bikini all day long.

"The logistics of an underwater wedding are a nightmare, but still, we managed to pull it together. The wedding party and all of the guests wore these masks that covered their whole faces and allowed them to both talk and hear others. Everyone strapped on their gear, and we all descended together." She smiled and shook her head. "I should point out that diving in the Caribbean is like diving in an aquarium. The water is clear and you can see for miles. The water in Lake Travis isn't that clear. That day, the visibility was about a foot, so you could only see as far as your own hand in front of you."

She started laughing and he'd never heard a better sound.

"Since we couldn't see each other, people were knocking into each other, and only about half of us made it to the platform at thirty feet. Luckily, the bride and groom made it. We waited and waited and waited, but no minister. Here's the thing about diving. If you're new to it, you use up your air a lot faster than an experienced diver, even at thirty feet, which is pretty shallow. Add in the commotion of one-foot visibility and the stress of bouncing off other divers and, well, people were running out of air and needed to start their ascent back to the surface. There were some people who were more experienced than others, so we weren't all running low on air, but the minister still hadn't shown up, so I went looking for him."

She took a deep breath and let it out slowly. "As it turns out, the number of ordained ministers who are open-water certified is pretty small. When I finally found one, I should have asked more questions, like how many dives he'd taken and how long ago he was certified. He'd gotten certified forty years ago and only had three dives under his belt, the last one being before I was born. When I finally found him, he was low on oxygen and his regulator hose was caught on a tree branch."

"A tree branch?" He wasn't aware trees grew underwater, but since it was Austin and they liked to keep things weird, anything was possible.

"Lake Travis is man-made. The Lower Colorado River Authority created it by flooding a canyon. It's to help with flooding and to provide water to Austin and the surrounding areas. There's a pecan grove and paved roads, and even a graveyard under the water." She laughed. "I found him freaked out and low on air. He was all of three feet under the surface. I tell myself that it was the bad visibility and not the stupidity of Reverend Dell Hamm, but deep down I know he's an idiot. All he needed was one fin kick, or even to raise his arm, and he would have broken the surface."

"Did the bride and groom end up getting married?" He

could almost see her giving that reverend a piece of her mind.

"No, as a matter of fact, they didn't. The bride took it as a sign from God that they shouldn't get married." She shrugged her shoulders. "Well, that and the fact that the groom was sleeping with her brother."

He laughed. "Only in Austin. I guess it's good she found out now instead of later." He couldn't imagine the bride had been too thrilled to find out that her husband was sleeping with her brother. "I bet family Thanksgiving was very interesting that year. What about the other almost drowning?"

"The other one wasn't all that spectacular." She put the washcloth she'd been using to clean into a wicker laundry hamper in the corner. "That had to do with a homemade boat dock on Lake Austin. The bride's great-grandfather had built it and it was where he'd proposed to her great-grandmother. I tried to explain that the janky hundred-year-old dock was a bad idea, but the bride was determined. The minister got halfway through the ceremony when the boards holding up the dock began to buckle and the whole wedding party slowly sank into Lake Austin. I should also mention that the groom and all of his seven groomsmen were professional wrestlers. I think their combined weight had something to do with the dock giving way. Honestly, seeing all fourteen attendants, two flower girls, the bride and groom, and the minister all on the old dock—I felt sorry for the dock. If I had to hold up all of that weight, I'd crater too."

A thought occurred to him. "Planning all of those weddings... I bet you've got yours planned all the way down to the honeymoon." Not that he minded her planning their wedding, but he'd like a heads-up so he knew what he was in for.

She chewed on her lower lip and then shook her head. "I've never really thought about my wedding. I can't really see myself as married." She shook her head like she was trying to picture it but couldn't quite wrap her mind around it.

"Why not?" His new personal goal was to change that.

"I don't know." It sounded like she honestly had never thought about it. "I guess I was so busy planning everyone else's wedding that I never really gave marriage any thought." She leaned against the counter and started folding and unfolding her arms again. Something was on her mind. "I put your clothes on to wash." She stared at the floor.

Sexual tension charged the air like static electricity.

"Thanks." What did it say about him that he was enjoying her discomfort? For once around her, he had the upper hand.

She brought her right hand to her mouth and chewed on her index fingernail and then realized she was biting her nails and purposefully dropped her hand. "I think we should talk about the kiss."

He mashed his lips together to keep from smiling and also to keep the soup from leaking out.

"We really need to talk about it." She rubbed her right index finger against her very rumpled skirt.

"What's there to say? I kissed you and you kissed me back. I enjoyed it and you enjoyed it. I think we'd both like for it to happen again." He spooned in another bite.

Her face scrunched up and three lines popped out on her forehead.

He could all but hear her brain working. It was like she was trying to recall all bazillion digits of pi.

"It's just... I mean... why did you kiss me?" She didn't sound mad, only contemplative.

"Why did you kiss me back? Matters of the heart are a mystery." He shot her his boyish smile. He'd been using it to disarm women ever since he was old enough to control his facial muscles.

"I... um... think it's chemistry." Her voice cracked, so she cleared her throat. Her right hand went to her mouth but changed course at the last minute and played with the neck-line of her prim-but-splotched-with-stains white shirt. "Why did you risk your life to find me?"

"I needed to make sure you were okay." It was lame and he knew it, but he wasn't sure the real answer was the best answer.

How did he best explain that he'd fallen in love with her about two seconds after setting eyes on her and that the thought of her in any sort of danger actually made him physically ill? He'd have gladly laid down his life to save her. He'd never thought of himself as chivalrous, but here he was being all chivalrous.

"Why?" Clearly, she knew it was lame too.

He guessed it was too soon to ask her to marry him or even to join him in the tub. "Why do you always wear your hair in that librarian bun? Don't get me wrong, I like it, but I'd love to see your hair down. I bet it's soft."

Did she notice the subject change?

She touched her falling-out-of-its-bun hair and watched him. "Your mom thinks you have a crush on me."

He didn't know what to say. He loved his mother, but right now he couldn't figure out why matricide was frowned upon.

Rosie fiddled with a loose strand of her bun. "I have to admit... I'm attracted to you." She sounded about as excited as if she'd just found out she had an STD.

"I'm attracted to you too." He shrugged. "It's good to

know I'm not in this one alone." He picked up the bottle of water, unscrewed the cap, and downed half of it. He set the bottle aside and scooped up another spoonful of soup.

"There's really only one way to handle this." Her arms folded against her chest, and for once they stayed there.

"What's that?" His heart ached horribly, because he knew what she was about to say next. It was bound to be some version of not mixing business with pleasure, or how their getting together would complicate things.

"I think we should have sex." With that she turned on her heel and walked out of the bathroom.

The spoon that was headed to his mouth bounced off his chin. Three noodles and a cube of chicken hit the water with a plop.

Of all the things that could have come out of her mouth, that wasn't something he'd expected. He smiled to himself. Rosie was turning out to be more surprising than he'd expected. That was why he loved her. Every single time he saw her, he learned something new about her. He'd never really been in love before. Was everything always... well, this rosy?

9

Rosie had no reckless moments in her life to regret, but admitting to Dallas that she wanted to sleep with him just might qualify.

She stirred her chicken noodle soup. Steam billowed up, so she turned the flame off and poured the soup into a white bowl. She laid the dirty pot in the sink and took her bowl to the two-seater bistro table next to the bay window.

How pathetic was it that mentioning she'd like to have sex with someone she barely knew was the most adventurous thing she'd ever done?

Boring people of the world, behold your queen. She waved to her imaginary royal subjects and then realized she was waving to imaginary people and let her arm drop to her side.

Sleeping with Dallas was bound to complicate her life, but maybe it needed a little complication. She was starting over here with the B&B, so why not take a complete departure from her normal life and have a torrid affair?

Trouble was, she didn't see herself as the torrid affair

kind of woman. She was more of the lukewarm, let's-go-dutch-for-dinner kind of girl.

"Rosie," Dallas called from the bathroom. "I hate to ask, but I need help getting out of the tub."

She scooped in a huge bite of soup, set her spoon down, and went to help him. He was naked. This was going to be awkward. She'd told him that she wanted to sleep with him, but she had no idea whether that was reciprocated. Now she felt her cheeks flame. Sex was turning out to be complicated.

Then again, when was it not?

"I'm coming." She opened the bathroom door and kept her eyes on the ceramic floor tiles. She could hear the water —and all of those bubbles—draining out of the tub.

"I hate that I have to ask for help." He sounded frustrated with himself.

"It is my fault you're injured." She stood next to the tub, not sure what she was supposed to do.

He was very darn naked. She was almost sure that gawking was a bad idea. Closing her eyes was a good idea. Yes, she should definitely close her eyes. She squeezed them shut.

"I'm just going to throw this out there, but in my opinion, you should keep your eyes open. I mean, on the best of days, I'm uncoordinated. One of us needs to have all of their faculties in working order." He touched her hand. "If it helps, you can take off your clothes so we're both naked. I promise to keep my eyes closed the whole time."

Her eyes fluttered open, and she caught his look-how-cute-I-am boyish smile. He had charm to spare and he knew it.

"Somehow, I think that's a bad idea." She grinned. "I

know that's contrary to my earlier statement, but for right now, I think my clothes should stay on."

She went to the linen closet and grabbed a towel. She unfolded it partway and laid it over his midsection.

"You want me. You know it and I know it." He waggled his eyebrows. "Let's cut the chitchat and get to the good stuff."

"So, you like to cut out the preliminaries and go straight to the big-ticket items?" She'd never been in a situation quite like this. "That doesn't sound like the generous and thorough lover I was hoping for."

That should take the wind out of his sails.

He scratched his head, clearly looking for a way to turn the situation around. Finally, he shook his head. "I got nothing... only that I promise once we're together, I'll spoil you for all other men."

"You've set the bar pretty high. I feel I should point out that there's no coming back from that. Either you've got to be Captain America, Loki, and Thor all rolled into one, or it's going to be a bust. I hate to dole out the tough love, but I gotta call them as I see them." She really enjoyed the dawning look of horror on his face.

He shook his head. "You can't have Loki qualities and Thor qualities in the same lover. They're polar opposites."

She shrugged. "What can I say, I like me a bad boy every now and then." She thought about it for a second. "I was going to throw in Dr. Xavier just to mix it up, but Patrick Stewart really was the best Dr. Xavier even though James McAvoy is way cuter."

He held his hands up in the universal stop gesture. "Now let's hold on. You can't cut a man out based on his advanced age. That's ageist. And I simply won't tolerate ageism in my presence."

"It has nothing to do with his age. It's more about *Star Trek: Next Gen*. Captain Picard had a thing for Dr. Crusher, and she was way too whiney and distant for my taste. A man that puts up with that crap is no man for me." She had to draw a line in the sand somewhere.

"Are you really a sci-fi geek or are you just trying to impress me?" He looked absolutely awed.

"Would I have all seven seasons of *Next Gen* on my iPad if all I wanted to do was impress you?" She looked down her nose at him. "I don't think so."

He put his hand over his heart and bowed his head. "I stand corrected, and I think I just fell in love with you." He winked.

"Your love protestations and your easy ability to change the subject won't make up for your earlier statement that you're going to ruin me for all other men." She shook her head. "You have a lot to live up to."

"Yeah, I really should have thought that out a little bit more." His eyes locked onto hers. "I don't suppose I could convince you to grade on the curve?"

She shook her head. "Nope. Once that bar is set, it's set in stone." She tilted her head to the left. "You might be able to talk me into a pass-fail situation, but I wouldn't get your hopes up."

"Tough crowd." He rolled his eyes. "You make one little comment and they hold it against you." The boyish grin was back. "I don't suppose you have anything else you'd like to *hold* against me?"

"Really?" She arched an eyebrow. "Somewhere, there's a cheesy old man with a sternum bush missing his craptastic pickup line."

"Again with the ageism. And hey, I meant that in a totally platonic, nonsexual way. It's not my fault you want my body and read more into it than was really there." He was all innocence.

She wasn't sure how she'd ever found him awkward or rude. "I thought you needed help getting out of the tub?" She mashed her lips together to keep from laughing. Someone had to keep them on task.

"I do. This naked body is getting cold." He waved his hand down his body. "I'm willing to sacrifice my dignity and take one for the team. If I stay in here any longer, I'm bound to get hypothermia. Trust me when I tell you that you don't want a lover with hypothermia. I'm only looking out for you. I don't think a prune-wrinkled, water-logged lover makes the best impression. You deserve me at my best." He made it sound like he only had her best interests at heart.

"Thank you." She couldn't help the smile.

"Thanks are not necessary." He held up a magnanimous hand. "That's just how I roll."

"So," she pointed in his general direction, "what's your plan?"

"Well, first, I think we need to have the monogamy talk, and after, I'm going to peel you out of those clothes. Then I'm going to make sweet love to you while the top fifty make-out songs play in the background. Since I'm a fantastic lover, the earth will move, cherubs will play violins, and you'll beg me not to stop." His eyes crinkled at the corners. "All other men will pale by comparison."

"Wow, again with the high expectations." She mashed her lips together to keep from laughing. "But I meant, what's your plan for getting out of the tub?"

"Yeah, the details. I'm more of a big-picture kinda guy, so I'll leave the deets to you." He made it sound like he was bestowing the highest honor on her.

"How about I stand behind you and lift you up? You can swing your good leg over the side and I'll help you get into a sitting position. After that, I'll help you hop to the bed." She really didn't see any other way to get him to the bed. She didn't have anything to fashion crutches out of, and there weren't any chairs with wheels in the house.

He thought about it for a second. "That works for me. But I have to warn you, many a woman has lost the power of speech at the sight of my fantastic naked body."

"I'm willing to take my chances." She stepped behind him, bent over, and slid her arms under his.

"I like a woman who lives on the edge." He was an excellent flirt.

"Good to know." She wasn't an excellent flirt. She'd known him for over a year, but she'd never seen this side of him.

"Are you going to tell me we're going on three and then lift me on one?" He looked over his shoulder at her.

"No, this is one of those times I'm actually going to count to three." She widened her stance and bent at the knee. "One, two, three."

She lifted him up, and the towel fell away as he turned his hips so that he was sitting on the edge of the tub.

She glanced down. "It's so odd. I can still speak."

"In my defense, that water was frigid." He reached around her and grabbed a folded white robe off the shelf next to the tub.

Thank God she'd had the presence of mind to stock the bathroom with robes.

He sat forward, balancing on his good leg, and slid the robe around his back and then tied it in front.

He put his hand over his heart. "If it were up to me, I'd

prance around naked, but I don't want to overwhelm you with my physical beauty."

"Thank God. There was a moment there when I thought I might be overwhelmed." She fanned herself. He really did have a wonderful body, but she wasn't about to tell him that. He already had more than his fair share of self-confidence.

"Overwhelmed is such an interesting word. You can be overwhelmed or underwhelmed, but can you just be whelmed?" His jaw set, and he bit down on his lower lip, apparently trying to will the pain to go away. He took a couple of deep breaths as he scooted to the edge of the tub.

"What does whelmed feel like?" She slid her arm around his waist. It looked like he was distracting himself by making conversation. "I guess it would be the status quo, and it doesn't make sense to stand around thinking, 'Hey, just now I'm whelmed.'"

He nodded. "Makes sense."

"On three—really on three this time—we're going to stand." She leaned into him, preparing to take his body weight. "One, two, three."

He stood, and she took his body weight. He was heavier than she'd thought. They hop-shuffled to the bedroom.

He stopped. "No, you take the bed. I'll take the sofa."

"You're injured. You're taking the bed, and there will be no more discussion." She used her it's-final tone.

His shoulders slumped, and she lost her footing and then found it at the last moment.

He let out a resigned sigh. "We can take turns. I'll take tonight and you take tomorrow."

She hadn't planned on spending more than one night here, but it made sense. Even if the rain stopped right now, it would take a couple of days for the water to crest and then recede. They had food and bottled water, but clothes were a different story. She only had the clothes on her back. And a bathrobe. At least there was that. It wasn't like she could wash and dry her business suit.

"Looks like you're trying to figure out a particularly hard math problem." A slow smile crept across his face. "Or are you trying to figure out the best way to have your way with me?"

"I like a lover who's fully functioning. A broken ankle might slow you down. After all of your buildup, I expect nothing but your best. Nothing halfway." While she wanted him, she didn't like the idea of causing him pain, and she couldn't think of a way to immobilize his ankle during sex. "Aren't you afraid of hurting your ankle even more?"

"Naw, it only hurts when I move it." With his free hand, he reached out and grabbed the iron bed frame.

Gently, she helped him lower himself onto the right side of the bed. "Wouldn't you have to move it around a little during sex?"

"Yeah, but it'd be worth it." He scooted back onto the pillows and cautiously swung his injured ankle onto the bed. "If you're so worried about hurting my ankle, I can cut it off with my pocket knife. Hell, who needs two ankles?"

"That seems a little drastic just to have sex." She went to the armoire, pulled out two extra pillows, and brought them to the bed. "I'm not going to lie. This is going to hurt."

She lifted his left leg at the knee and slid the pillows under his foot.

"Actually, it wasn't that bad." His voice was at least an octave higher than normal, and he bit down on his bottom lip.

"Liar." She stepped back. There was one fatal flaw in her

plan. She hadn't turned down the bed, so there was no way of getting him under the comforter without moving his leg.

"Maybe I can roll on my side and you can pull the covers down." Clearly, he was thinking the same thing.

"Need some help?" She wasn't sure how he was going to roll on his side without hurting himself.

"You grab the covers and pull them down as soon as I roll over." As his face twisted in pain, he took two deep breaths and rolled onto his left side.

She yanked the covers down around him, careful to place them gently over his left foot.

He rolled onto his right side, and she yanked the covers down.

She pulled the comforter up to his chest.

He patted the other side of the queen bed. "Why don't you grab your soup and join me?"

"I can't." There was no eating in bed. That would be absurd. Her oldest sister had forbidden anyone from eating in bed. It was messy, and Louisa abhorred mess and clutter of any kind. Everything about her was no-nonsense, from her clothes to her choice of furnishings—function reigned and form didn't exist.

"Why not?" He looked like he was trying to figure out why but wasn't having any luck.

"Eating in bed is messy and..." And why couldn't she? Her sister wasn't around to comment. Heck, she hadn't lived with her sisters in several years.

"Lots of things are messy, but that shouldn't stop you from doing them." He put a hand to his chest. "I take pride in being messy. It's just part of my charm."

"Keep telling yourself that and maybe it'll come true." Why couldn't she eat in bed, just this once? She headed toward the kitchen, but her curiosity couldn't wait. "What's the messiest thing you've ever done?"

She grabbed her bowl, spoon, and napkin and hurried back to the bedroom.

"You're going to have to narrow it down. Are you talking about the messiest thing I've done with paint or food or explosives or all of the above? I take mess making seriously." There was absolutely no apology in his voice.

She didn't know that messes had to have qualifiers. "With paint."

"That would have to be Paintball Twister. That was a huge mess. Fortunately for me, I set it up inside Worth's house. I'm not sure he'll ever get all of that hot-pink paint out of the nooks and crannies." He seemed particularly proud of those pink-painted nooks and crannies.

She eased onto the bed, trying not to shake the mattress. "I can't even imagine. My oldest sister, Louisa, would have a stroke at the mention of Paintball Twister. She's a neat freak." She thought about it for a second. "All of my sisters are."

"How come they've never been to the ranch? You've been here off and on for over a year. Why don't they come to visit you?" He played with a stray string on the pale-green comforter.

"I don't think I've ever asked them. It never occurred to me." Everyone in her family had always been about the work. Yes, they saw each other frequently, but they never really talked about anything but work.

"You should have them come out and show them what you've built here. I'm sure they're very proud of you." He was so blasé about it. His family was always proud of him, so he took it for granted. Not that her sisters weren't proud of her, but they'd never told her. Talk of feelings, or even chitchat, was viewed as a waste of perfectly good time. And if there was something Louisa hated more than mess or laziness, it was wasting time.

Family made life complicated. Surely he of all people understood that.

10

D allas laced his fingers behind his head and couldn't get enough of Rosie. He was attracted to her, and he was in love with her, but he hadn't expected to like her so much. Now that he thought about it, that didn't make much sense. Of course he would like her, but he also enjoyed hanging out with her.

Their sci-fi common ground was an unexpected pleasure. They were polar opposites in some ways and polar sames in others. She really did love *Star Trek: Next Gen* enough to have all the episodes on her iPad. They'd just finished watching "Encounter at Farpoint" parts one and two.

"I'd forgotten how cheesy the effects were." He still couldn't believe he was sitting here next to Rosie and he was able to speak coherently. If his family could only see him now. To think, not twelve hours ago she'd seen him drool. On second thought, he didn't want to think of that ever again.

She hunched a shoulder. "It was 1987, so we can't fault them too much. Still, the command consoles move every

time someone touches them. The costumes are interesting."
She'd found a half gallon of Blue Bell Homemade Vanilla in
the freezer and had dished up two generous helpings. She
swirled her spoon in the ice cream and delicately licked the
small bite.

Whoever had packed the backpack he'd crossed the
river with had the presence of mind to throw in a pair of
black yoga pants and a red T-shirt, which Rosie was now
wearing. She'd taken a shower, and her long, thick black
hair was still damp, streaming down her back.

Whether she'd worn it down for him or because it was
easier to dry, it didn't matter. He was choosing to believe she
was wearing it down for him.

He'd never seen anyone savor ice cream more. His ice
cream was long gone, while she ate hers slowly. It might be
next Tuesday before she finished.

"I haven't watched these in a very long time. It feels like
they haven't found their groove yet." She used her spoon to
point at her iPad screen. "It's a work in progress."

"Everyone was so young." It had not escaped his notice
that she wasn't wearing a bra. His eyes wondered south to
the black yoga pants. Was she going commando too?

He licked his lips and then realized he was licking his
lips and mashed his lips together.

"If memory serves, the series really didn't find itself until
the middle of season two or the beginning of season three."
She swirled her spoon in the ice cream and brought another
tiny bite to her lips.

Did she eat everything this slowly? He didn't remember
her taking this kind of time eating her soup. It wasn't exactly
annoying so much as interesting. Swirl and then lick. Swirl
and then lick. She did everything fast except this. Swirl and
then lick.

"What are your feelings on *Farscape*?" Not that it was a deal breaker, but he wanted to know just how far her love of sci-fi went.

"Love it. Although, I can't get my head around the characters living inside a living ship. So, they all live inside Moya's stomach? That's really the only complaint I have about the show." Swirl and then lick. "Except that it was canceled."

Now it was time to bring in the deal breaker. " *Firefly*?"

He held his breath waiting for her answer.

"It's my favorite show ever. The only complaint I have is that it ended so abruptly. Joss Whedon is a god." Swirl and then lick. "The movie was wonderful. I hear there's going to be another one. Then again, that rumor has been circulating for years."

"I can't wait." He rolled his eyes. "God knows, *Star Wars* is such a disappointment. Well, *Rogue One* was entertaining. *The Force Awakens* was just *A New Hope* with different character names."

"I know what you mean. It was like they took the script for *A New Hope*, changed the names and locations, but used the same formula." She pointed to him with her spoon. "What's your favorite guilty-pleasure film?"

That was easy. " *Galaxy Quest*."

Her blue eyes went huge. "Mine too. Never give up. Never surrender."

She was too good to be true.

"What's your favorite part?" He wasn't quizzing her so much as confirming that they were made for each other.

"So many things. I love when Tawny is repeating what the rest of the crew is saying so that the computer will respond. She says, 'Look, I have one lousy job on this ship, it's stupid, but I'm going to do it.'"

"I like when they're on the planet and Tim Allen starts dive-rolling like they do on TV when there's a shoot-out and the person's trying to avoid getting shot." He still couldn't believe they had so much in common. "FYI—dive-rolling is strictly a Hollywood thing. Not that I've been in many shoot-outs, but I can't see how rolling would make any difference."

Slowly, her head turned toward him. "If you haven't been in many shoot-outs... doesn't that imply that you've been in some? How many?"

"Not real shoot-outs—just the paintball kind. Worth and I shoot it out every once in a while. We're teaching Hugh. He's got some skills." The boy definitely showed promise at paintball. He and Worth had stopped going easy on the kid, but he was still better than them.

"You and Worth fight a lot." She didn't sound upset, only making an observation.

"It all started in the womb when he wrapped his legs around my neck." He held a hand up. "I swear to God, he takes up more room than any other person alive. We may look the same, but we are very different people."

"I know. It didn't take me long to see the differences between you." She turned to look at him. "Yes, you look alike, but there are differences." She pursed her lips in what he was learning was her thinking pose. "Your faces are the same, but everything else about you is different. It's interesting, you have matching DNA, but your mannerisms, the way you conduct yourselves, is completely different." She nodded. "Even if you dressed the same, I'd still be able to tell the difference."

That made him smile. Now all he needed to know was how she felt about his brother. If she had romantic feelings for Worth, he'd bow out. Well, he'd have to kill his brother and then bow out, but he was a gentleman, so he'd do the right thing and kill him quickly.

"Don't you fight with your sisters?" He'd never had a sister—well, until CanDee and Justus. They gave good advice. It might have been nice to grow up with one.

"Yes, but we never hit each other." Swirl and lick.

"You're girls. Y'all probably do worse things." There was nothing worse than a girl fight. With men, there were rules, but girl fights didn't seem to have any.

She thought about it. "You're probably right. After my mother died, my sisters and I moved in with my oldest sister, Louisa. She lived in a one-bedroom apartment. Things were tight, space-wise and financially. My sisters were always at each other's throats. They did some pretty mean things to each other."

"How about you?" Surely she had some killer good-sister revenge stories.

"I was ten when my mother died, and I was the baby. They pretty much left me alone." She finally finished her ice cream and set the bowl on the nightstand.

He didn't detect hurt in her voice; in fact he didn't detect anything.

"Losing your mother at an early age, it must have been difficult." He wasn't prying so much as getting to know her.

She drew her knees up to her chest and wrapped her arms around them. "It was hard."

He waited for her to elaborate, but she clearly didn't have much to say on the subject.

"I can't imagine." He wasn't a quitter and was giving it another try. "How did she die?"

"Heart attack." She rested her chin on her knees. She'd drawn herself up into a ball. "My mother had... issues."

"Health issues? What kind?" In the last few hours they'd

talked about a lot of stuff, but nothing as important or as personal as this. He wanted to scratch the surface and see what was underneath.

She looked him dead in the eye. "She was in and out of rehab. Right before she died, she was diagnosed with bipolar disorder."

"What about your father?" Why hadn't her father taken her in after her mother had died?

She shook her head. "I don't know him. Never met him. My mother wasn't exactly sure which of the men she'd slept with was my father."

"That must have been hard, growing up without a father." Or a mother. He didn't need to point that out, since they'd just covered it.

She hunched a shoulder. "I guess. I don't really know."

"What's your favorite memory of childhood?" He knew he was pressing, but she wasn't exactly being forthcoming. It was odd. Usually, he was the first one to shy away from emotional conversations, but he wanted to know how she ticked and what made her the person she was.

She shook her head. "I don't know."

She picked up her iPad and propped it back on the pillow between them. "Want to watch the next episode?"

That was a big, fat, I-don't-want-to-talk reply if he'd ever heard one. It seemed that he'd gotten all he would get from her for now. "Sure."

She cued up episode three and set the iPad between them.

Outside, the storm raged on.

Maybe someday she'd trust him enough to talk about her past. Right now, it was enough that she was safe and they were together.

11

Two hours later, Rosie stood at the sink washing the dishes. She scrubbed the soup pan with a sponge she'd found under the sink.

It wasn't that she didn't want to talk about her past with Dallas... Okay, she really didn't want to talk about her past... with anyone.

In her experience, the past wasn't something to be remembered, it was something to be overcome.

Dallas had a loving mother and a loving father. She doubted he could understand what her childhood had been like.

Talking about her mother only made her feel guilty. As a child, Rosie had understood from the very beginning that she hadn't been wanted.

By the time her mother had realized she was pregnant with Rosie, it had been too late for an abortion. Rosie knew that her mother would have gotten rid of her if she could have, because her mother had told her so every chance she'd gotten. Even now, the hurt was so raw and painful that she couldn't talk about it to anyone. She'd ruined her mother's life. And she'd worked harder and longer than anyone, trying to make up for it.

Tears burned her eyes, and she angrily swiped them away. Tears were useless things, and she detested herself for crying over a crappy childhood. Everyone thought their childhood was crappy. She needed to get over it. No one wanted to hear her sob story. Even she didn't want to go over the details any longer, but here she was hashing out the low points.

It wasn't fair, but then again, life wasn't fair, so bitching about it wouldn't change a thing. She'd tried so hard not to be a burden on her mother or her sisters, but she'd failed time and time again.

She remembered so clearly sitting in the closet trying to be quiet while her mother and her current boyfriend were having some "private time" in the one-bedroom apartment she shared with her mother and sisters. Rosie had only been five, or maybe six, and her sisters had been old enough to be out with friends all the time. She'd been in that closet for hours, and she'd needed to use the bathroom. She'd waited as long as she could, but she had to open the door and head to the bathroom.

Her mother had whipped her so hard she'd wet her pants. She'd tried so hard to be good, but she was never good enough.

Tears came harder for the little girl who hadn't been wanted.

Rarely did she let herself wallow in self-pity, but sometimes it snuck up on her and put her in a choke hold. She scrubbed the pot harder, as if she could scrub away the hurt.

Logically, the adult version of herself knew that her mother was the problem and not her, but the little girl who just wanted to be loved still lived inside her.

She'd gone from her mother's hatred to her sister's cold-ness. At least Louisa didn't hate her. That was something. But her sister had ruled with an iron fist. Hugs hadn't been part of her childhood, so they didn't have a place in her adulthood.

When it came to family, there wasn't any warmth, just obligation.

Dallas's family had warmth down to a science. She loved watching them together. Hugs were easy, and smiles came often. She was getting used to it. She thought of CanDee and Justus and now Lucy as her family.

Even Justus and CanDee didn't know her deepest, darkest secrets. She hadn't purposefully kept them from them, she just wasn't that much into sharing. Her first Christmas at Texas State, rooming with CanDee and Justus, had been an eye-opener. She'd spent Christmas Eve at Justus's house.

They'd had a big family Christmas with presents and turkey and all of the trimmings. They'd opened presents on Christmas Eve and speculated about what Santa Claus would bring them. It was lovely and sweet and weird as hell.

CanDee and her grandmother had been there, and they seemed to understand all of that Christmas cheer. Rosie remembered sitting on the sofa just watching all of the smiles and laughter. It was, for lack of a better word, over-whelming.

There had been a stocking for Rosie hanging next to the one for CanDee. Justus's stepmother had sewed their names on the stockings, like they were official family members. Maeve, Justus's stepmother, had made a big deal of how the stockings had to be out so Santa Claus could fill them.

Rosie had been all of four years old when she'd figured out that Santa Claus was a hoax. All of that wishing and hoping for a toy to show up was just a waste of perfectly good time. Waking up heartbroken on Christmas morning had taught her the truth about Santa. Things had been a little better after she'd moved in with her sisters. They always managed to buy each other little presents. Nothing frivolous, always something that was needed, but it was nice to open a wrapped present on Christmas morning.

On the few occasions her mother had been sober enough to notice that it was Christmas, she'd signed Rosie up for the Angel Tree or Blue Santa, but the presents she got were always confiscated by her mother and sold or traded for drugs.

Because Rosie knew exactly how it felt to wake up to nothing on Christmas morning, these days she always took several names off of the Angel Tree and carefully shopped, wrapped, and delivered the gifts. She chose to believe that the children receiving those gifts got to keep them.

A loud crash, like glass breaking, came from the bedroom. She tossed the sponge in the sink and ran to check on Dallas.

He was leaning over the side of the bed, trying to pick up white shards of his broken ice cream bowl.

"I'll get that." She slid into the black Jimmy Choos she'd left by the bedroom door.

"Sorry. I'm a klutz. I was going for the water bottle and I knocked over the bowl." He was all contrite little boy.

"No worries. I would have picked it up when I left the room, but you were sleeping and I didn't want to wake you.

Careful not to step on the broken bits, she picked up the large pieces. She brought them to the kitchen and dumped them in the trash under the sink. She grabbed the hand-broom and dustpan next to the trash can and went to finish the clean up.

"I wish I could be more help." He sounded frustrated with himself and the situation.

"It wasn't your fault. You need to rest and stay off of your ankle." She brushed the last of the bowl bits into the dustpan. "You finished your second helping of ice cream just a little while ago. It's probably a good time for another dose of ibuprofen."

"Thanks. It doesn't hurt now, but I'd like to keep ahead of the pain." He lay back against the pillows.

She dumped the contents of the dustpan into the trash, grabbed the ibuprofen, and headed back into the bedroom.

"You're supposed to take two." She upended the bottle and shook out two pills. She handed them to him and then picked up the bottle of water on the nightstand next to him, waited for him to pop the pills in his mouth, unscrewed the water, and handed it to him.

He downed the rest of the bottle.

"Want another?" She took the empty bottle.

"No, I'm good." His eyes zeroed in on hers. "Your eyes are swollen and red. Have you been crying?"

Life had been so much easier when he'd been a drooler.

"Yes." She wasn't a coward. She threw her shoulders back and straightened her spine.

"Why?" He patted the side of the bed where she'd been sitting not two hours ago. "Is it the storm? I'm sure we'll get out of here soon."

"What?" She shook her head. "No, it's just a storm. I find it weirdly comforting. No, you'd asked about my past, which got me thinking about my mother."

"Sorry, I bet you miss her. It was very insensitive of me." He looked down at the pale-green comforter. "I didn't mean to make you sad."

"It's not that. I don't miss my mother, exactly." How

could she make him understand? He didn't have the frame of reference to fully get her situation. Then again, she shouldn't make assumptions about what he could or couldn't understand. "My childhood was pretty bad. My mother had issues with drugs."

"Prescription drugs?" He really didn't understand.

"No... well, yes, if she came into some money and could afford them." She propped one knee on the edge of the bed. "She did... a lot of different stuff. Basically whatever she could get her hands on. She wasn't picky."

He just sat there with his mouth hanging open for several beats.

She knew what was next. It would be pity. Pity was actually worse than her childhood, which was saying something.

"It's okay," she said. "I know you can't relate." She was more than ready to drop the subject.

He recovered and watched her very carefully. "Why?"

"Why what?" She longed to escape to the living room, but she kept her back ramrod straight.

"Why was she on drugs?" He made it sound like the most logical question in the world.

That question threw her. She'd never had anyone ask it.

"Addiction is a disease." She gave him the pat answer that TV psychologists loved to throw out. Part of her knew she was the reason her mother couldn't face reality.

"I can tell by the look on your face that you don't believe that." He yawned.

"It looks like I'm keeping you from resting." She stood.

He grinned. "No you don't. Stay right there. I'm the only one who gets to change the subject when I don't want to talk about something."

"Noticed that, did you?" She returned the grin.

He laced his fingers behind his head and leaned back against the pillows. "Yes, ma'am, I sure did."

She climbed onto the bed and sat next to him. "Many years after she died, I found out from one of my sisters that our mother had been diagnosed with bipolar disorder. The prevailing theory is that she had been self-medicating."

"I get the feeling that you don't agree." He continued to watch her.

"Sure, why not? She had bipolar—that makes sense. It also could have been that she was weak or hated her life or had some genetic predisposition for substance abuse, or she could have just liked the way it made her feel. Does it matter why she did it?" The last sentence came out really loud. She hadn't meant to shout, but she was shouting all the same. She took a deep breath. "Sorry."

She didn't want to have to admit that she was the reason her mother preferred to be high.

"You have nothing to apologize for. I'm the one who wouldn't let it go. I'm sorry." He reached out and took her hand. "I don't understand addiction either. Yes, I think it's a disease, but I also think that people need to take some responsibility for their actions. In this day and age, it seems that everyone blames their mistakes on someone else rather than noticing that they are the common denominator."

"I feel the same way." Well, mostly. "Also, there is some physiological component to it too. The body becomes dependent on the drug and can't live without it." That had been one of her mother's many justifications for selling Rosie's meager possessions to get high. The most popular way her mother justified her addiction was to say she was "sick." Some of Rosie's earliest memories were of watching her mother sleeping passed out on the floor and trying to wake her up, or cleaning up her mother's vomit from before she'd passed out. That was a lot to put on a child.

She opened her mouth to change the subject, but instead every single detail of her childhood came out. She left nothing out. She told him about her earliest memories of watching her mother "cook" heroin and lace cigarettes with PCP and LSD. And how she learned from the age of four to hide from her mother as she became paranoid coming down off of crystal meth. Or the time she'd had to sing in the school performance in only her stockings, because her mother had sold her only nice shoes to buy drugs.

She'd never told anyone—not even her sisters or her best friends—everything about her childhood, but it was all coming out. Her voice was so hollow, it should have had an echo, but she soldiered on through her terrible memories. It sounded like she was recounting someone else's life.

When she was finished, she took a deep, cleansing breath and let it out slowly. It felt like a weight had been lifted off her chest. She'd always thought that talking about it would make it worse, but she was finding that the opposite was true. Sharing the burden seemed to lessen the load.

Dallas laced his fingers through hers, brought her hand up to his mouth, and kissed it. "You're the bravest person I've ever met."

She'd expected pity, but all she saw on his face was awe. He really thought she was brave to have made it through her childhood.

Was she brave? She'd never really thought of herself as brave. She guessed she was a survivor. Addiction was most definitely not a victimless crime. It affected the lives of every single person who came into contact with the addict.

"I'm not sure 'brave' is the right word." When she was in

the situation, there hadn't been a decision to be brave; it had just been her life.

"How about 'survivor'? It takes a very strong person to come through something like that and not let it destroy their future." There certainly wasn't an ounce of pity in him.

"Thanks." Now that she thought about it, she really was a strong person. Somehow she'd survived her awful childhood and come out okay on the other side.

She was a survivor. That was a whole lot better than being a victim or perpetrator.

12

D allas gritted his teeth as he rolled onto his side and faced Rosie.

"You've shared something private with me, and now I feel l should share something private with you." He didn't know how he knew, but he just knew that she needed a good laugh. She was retreating into herself, and too much self-reflection was always a bad idea.

She inched down the bed and lay on her side facing him.

She was all wide, solemn blue eyes. "Okay."

"It's really more of a confession." He wanted the buildup. The bigger the buildup, the bigger the laugh.

Her brow scrunched up and she covered his hand with hers. "You can tell me anything."

"It's pretty shocking. Are you ready?" He put on his brave face. "In the fifth grade, I convinced my baby brother, T-Bone, that he was radioactive and that if anyone touched him they would die. Did you know that you can order radiation suits on Amazon?"

She looked confused, and then the story registered and she threw her head back and laughed.

The sound made his soul smile.

"Then I convinced him that Worth and I were wizards who secretly went to Hogwarts but that after we—Worth and I, that is, and not Harry Potter—were the ones to defeat Voldemort, we were too famous to live among the magically inclined. He honestly believed that we were in some sort of wizarding witness-relocation program so we were forced to live with muggles." Dallas shook his head. "He was so disappointed when he didn't get a letter from Hogwarts."

She was laughing so hard that tears were rolling down her cheeks. "What else?"

"Well, let me see..." He scratched his chin. He was fully prepared to make up things, but sadly, fiction was more believable than the truth. "We convinced T-Bone he could fly. We had him jump off the roof to get momentum. He broke his ankle. We felt bad."

"I bet your parents were mad." Her eyes sparkled when she smiled.

Did his eyes sparkle when he smiled? Come to think of it, sparkly eyes were something girls noticed.

Damn, he was turning into a girl. He caught himself before he rolled his eyes.

"You have no idea. It's the only time I ever saw my dad lose it. Usually, my mom was the one to discipline us, because my dad is a big softy. He'd waggle his finger at us and say, 'Wait until your mother gets home.' That time I really thought he was going to kill us." It had been both frightening and hilarious.

"What was your punishment?" She wanted to know about his life. It was a start.

"I don't remember, but T-Bone played it up. I'm

convinced that he really didn't need those crutches but only did it for the attention." His baby brother had always been a drama queen. Now that he'd probably broken his ankle, Dallas was willing to concede that T-Bone might actually have needed those crutches.

He scratched his chin again. "Now that I think about it, T-Bone's pretty gullible. It's a wonder that he made it to adulthood."

"I don't really have any funny stories about my sisters. All I remember was them working hard to keep a roof over our heads. Now that their company is established, they don't have to work so hard, but they do anyway." There was pride in her voice.

"What company? What's the family business?" He really should ask her more personal questions. It seemed that he had spent what little time he'd been able to speak to her talking about himself.

A lock of her hair fell across her face and she tucked it behind her ear. "They started Fantastic Flans."

"Don't toy with me woman." Up until now, he hadn't believed in soul mates, but he'd just changed his mind. "Their dulce de leche flan is hands down the best thing I've ever tasted."

"That's my favorite too," she said. "Yep, my sisters own Fantastic Flans."

He took both of her hands in his. "I have a very important question to ask you. I'd get down on one knee, but I can't. So... here goes. Will you marry me?"

He was only half kidding.

She busted out laughing. "Marriage seems a little extreme just for free flan."

"I was hoping for a discount, but free? I'd be willing to give birth to our children for free flan." He let go of her left hand and tilted her chin up. He laid his lips on hers for just a taste and then he pulled back.

He was enjoying the dazed look on her face. He felt exactly the same way. "There's a lot I'd do for free flan, but marrying you seems like the most pleasant."

"Words every girl waits a lifetime to hear." She grinned.

For someone who'd spent most of her adult life planning weddings, she didn't seem the mushy-gushy hearts and flowers type of girl.

"For the sake of argument, let's say that you did agree to marry me. I bet you really do have your wedding planned to the millisecond."

Confusion settled on her face. "Didn't we already talk about my wedding?" She shook her head. "I have no idea about it."

"I don't believe that. I bet you have everything planned." He could see right through her. If she were a Barbie, she'd be Work Her Fingers to the Bone Barbie.

"Honestly, I don't see myself ever getting married." Her words didn't sound like they were coming from a place of anger. She was just stating a fact.

"You don't believe in marriage?" He was having a hard time buying that one. Anyone who spent as much time planning the perfect day as she did had to believe in marriage.

"That's not it. At least, I don't think that's it. I've just never really thought of myself as marriage material." By the look on her face, she really believed it. "I'm fairly certain I'd end up in the fifty percent of marriages that end in divorce." She thought about it for a second. "In fact, I can usually tell which couples will make it and which ones won't."

"How?" He didn't agree with her about her marriage

prospects, but arguing about it wasn't going to get him anywhere.

"I can always tell when a couple is going through the motions instead of truly caring about each other. It all starts with the gift." She tucked another stray lock of hair behind her ear.

Her hair looked so soft he wanted to touch it, but it would ruin the mood.

"What gift?" He had no idea what wedding protocol was, much less what gift she was talking about.

"It's customary for the bride and groom to exchange gifts right before the wedding. I can always tell by the gift whether the marriage will last." She grabbed the pillow behind her, balled it up, and laid her head down on it.

"What? Is it based on money or something?" He had lots of money, so buying her a wedding present that sparkled wouldn't be a problem. Only, she didn't seem like the type of woman who wanted big, flashy jewelry.

"No, in fact it's the opposite." She tucked her hand under the pillow, and he was willing to bet that she was a side sleeper.

He sent up a prayer to God that he'd find out tonight. Should he actually be praying for sex? Somehow it seemed wrong.

She continued. "The average cost of a wedding in the United States is a little over thirty-five thousand dollars. I see couples breaking the bank for their wedding and then buying really expensive presents for each other. When I see a groom pull out a pair of huge diamond earrings or some bracelet that costs more than the wedding, mentally, I usually give them less than five years."

"Why?" He'd bought many a flashy bobble for a girl-friend. Come to think of it, none of those relationships had lasted very long. Then again, none of those women had been Rosie. He hadn't wanted permanence until her.

"Because if you have to buy someone's affection, it isn't real. Love is free. Diamond earrings might appease her for now, but what about tomorrow? And what about when she finds someone who can buy her even bigger diamond earrings?" She smiled to herself, and her eyes softened like she was remembering something wonderful. "The best gifts are thoughtful ones, and usually they don't cost much."

"Like what?" He was prepared to ply her for information all night if he had to. He wanted to know everything about her, and all it had cost him was a broken ankle. It was a hell of a deal.

"It's the gifts from the heart." She rolled her eyes. "I don't mean cheesy poetry. I can always tell the couples who will stay together, because they know each other so well. They are beyond buying the gifts they want the other person to have and instead buy the gifts the other person really wants."

"I don't understand. Isn't it the same thing?" Wow, he'd never realized how complicated weddings were. Had Rowdy and Justus exchanged gifts? Did Cinco know he was supposed to buy a gift for CanDee? Should he tell Cinco he needed to give his fiancée a thoughtful gift before the wedding, or should he just keep quiet and watch his older brother flounder?

Floundering sounded like way more fun.

"For example, I had a boyfriend once who thought I loved expensive crystal figurines." She shook her head. "I don't know where he got that idea, but he was forever giving me those delicate little things." She swept a hand down her body. "What part of me says that I love crystal figurines?"

She was right. She was all about the no-nonsense. Two

seconds after meeting her, he'd known she wasn't a frilly kinda girl. Something about that really turned him on. Maybe it was the desire to find whatever frills she had locked inside, or maybe he just appreciated the way she took nothing for granted and went after whatever she wanted. Either way, he was so into Rosie.

"Nothing about you screams figurines." What he knew of her was practical to the core. There was no room for figurines.

"Exactly. Rather than take the time to get to know me, he decided I was a figurines kinda girl, so he bought me what he wanted me to have instead of what I like." She held a hand up. "I don't want to come off as materialistic, because I'm really not. All I'm trying to say is that if you're contemplating spending the rest of your life with someone, shouldn't you know them well enough to know they don't like crystal figurines?"

"Makes sense." He'd never really thought about it before, but she was right. If he was going to spend the rest of his life with Rosie, he needed to get to know her pretty damn quick. No crystal figurines... got it. "What are some of the best presents you've seen brides and grooms exchange?"

Surely she would throw in a couple of her own favorite things.

The smile was back, making her eyes sparkle. "Once, I had a bride who bought her groom monster truck rally tickets. I thought it was a terrible gift until I saw his eyes light up. Another time, I had a groom from very old Dallas money. His wife was from a working-class family. He knew that she was worried about how her family would fit in the big, fancy wedding his parents were pushing on them. So two days before the wedding, the groom called every single guest and told them that the wedding was casual and asked them to please wear jeans. Thank God he didn't tell me until after the wedding, because I would have advised him against it, but as the bride walked down the aisle she knew immediately what he'd done for her. The awe and love on her face was breathtaking."

Her face had softened, and he saw the very first sign of frilly. She loved the love part of the wedding. It was funny, he hadn't taken her for an emotional girl, but deep down, he could see that she was.

"What else?" He wanted for her to get personal. He wanted to know what he could do for her that would matter the most.

She shook her head. "I don't know. There are the sweet gifts, like love letters or an empty photo album that the couple can fill with memories, or the family heirloom that's passed down. And then there are the strange gifts."

"Stranger than monster truck rally tickets?" He'd actually like monster truck rally tickets.

"Oh yeah. Some of the weird gifts off the top of my head: a 1960s lava lamp, a picture of J. Edgar Hoover in drag, a surprise honeymoon in a haunted jail, and a truckload of watermelons." She looked like she couldn't fathom why anyone would want those things. "There was a two-hundred-year-old fruitcake that had some meaning to the groom, but my favorite was the matching engraved axes."

"Axes, like chopping-things-down axes?" He didn't know much about weddings, but axes didn't seem like a good idea.

"The bride and groom gave each other matching ice axes for climbing Mt. Everest." She touched his hand. "You might think they were going to climb Everest on their honeymoon, but no. Both were in their upper sixties, and one was in a wheelchair."

"What was with the axes?" Given the wedding couple's physical limitations, it just seemed like a bad idea.

She shook her head. "Don't know, but they were both teary eyed when I delivered their presents."

Emo over ice axes... to each his own.

"What would you want as your special wedding-day present from your groom?" Blatant much? He was tired of talking around the point. He really wanted to know.

She shook her head. "That's just it. It should be something I don't know I've always wanted."

No pressure there. How in the hell was he supposed to figure that out when she didn't even know she wanted it?

He was coming to the conclusion that weddings were more complicated than just a couple of people wearing fancy clothes and saying, "I do."

He didn't want to downplay her career, but a wedding was just one day. How could that be so complicated?

"I find it hard to believe that you don't have a general idea of what you'd like on your wedding day." He didn't want to push too hard, but he really wanted to know what he was in for. He refused to believe that they wouldn't end up together.

Come on, she had to have something in mind.

She shrugged. "For the sake of argument, let's say I do find someone who doesn't get on my nerves and that I could stand to be with for more than like one month. I guess I'd want something simple. On my wedding day, I'd like to get up, put on the simple white dress I've bought for the occasion, fix my own hair, and meet my husband by the river or in an open field on a sunny, cloudless day. I'd like to get married outside—which, by the way, is a nightmare to plan, but I don't care. I want no frills. I just want a couple of friends, some family, and an easy, fun day. No caterers or florists or DJs. Just a simple ceremony followed by a picnic."

He had to say that sounded really good to him too. Not that he'd ever really thought about getting married... well, until he'd met Rosie. But an outdoor wedding with just family and friends on a cloudless day was just about perfect. "I like your version of a wedding."

"Me too." She smiled to herself. "Thanks for making me think of it."

"Now let's talk about your fiancé. Your only requirement is that he not get on your nerves so you can stand him for more than one month." He did his best to keep his voice light and not like he was taking mental notes. "What exactly are the things that men have done that get on your nerves?"

She sighed long and hard. "I don't have a list per se. I guess it's on a person-by-person basis. My last boyfriend, Zane, overused the word 'like.' Every other word out of his mouth was 'like.' Everything was 'like this way' or 'I was thinking like we could like...' Even though he was a couple of years older than me, I felt like I was babysitting but I wasn't getting paid."

"I know what you mean. I dated this girl, Kelsey, she 'liked' every sentence to death. It got to the point that I didn't want to have a conversation with her because of all of those likes." In the end, he'd started counting the number of likes per conversation. Her record was two hundred and eighty-four.

"I know what you mean." She yawned. "I stopped answering his texts because he over-liked in those too. In my mind, I charged him twenty-five cents a like." She did some mental math. "I figure he owes me somewhere in the neighborhood of five hundred million dollars. Maybe I should send him a bill?"

He nodded. "I think that's reasonable."

She yawned again.

He glanced around for a clock but didn't find one. It had to be late. He reached behind him and turned off the bedside lamp.

She made as if to get up, but he put a hand on her shoulder. "Stay. We can sleep in the same bed. I promise to be a perfect gentleman. Then again, you want my body, so maybe I should be worried." He yawned.

"I'll try to control myself." She added a long stretch to her yawn and then rolled over onto her right side so that her back was facing him.

His hands itched to touch her, but he'd promised. He didn't recall ever just sleeping beside a woman... well, only if he fell asleep after sex. There was something comforting about just being near her. She was close enough that he could smell the lemony shampoo on her hair.

He couldn't wait to wake up beside her.

13

"Damn." The whispered word startled Rosie awake.

"What?" She sat up and tried to remember where she was. When she fell asleep, she was out for a good nine hours. Any interruption in her sleep cycle was usually met with outrage and confusion—always in that order.

"Sorry, I was trying to get up without waking you," a male voice said.

She looked around, but it was so dark.

Thoughts crashed through her brain. She was in the Villa with Dallas Rose, and he'd hurt himself making sure she was safe.

"Are you okay? Is it your ankle?" Her eyes were beginning to adjust to being open. She felt around on the bed for him, but all she got were cold, empty sheets. "Where are you?"

She knew he was close, but she had no sense of where.

He gritted out an embarrassed breath. "I'm on the floor. I tried to hobble quietly to the bathroom, but I tripped over the nightstand." He heaved and the mattress jerked like he was using it to help himself up. "I'm pretty sure I took out the lamp. I have to say, when you fall asleep, bombs exploding in the front yard couldn't wake you. That's impressive."

He did sound very impressed.

"Thanks... I think." She slid off the bed and went to help him. She rounded the bed and stopped short. "Is there any broken glass?"

She wouldn't be any help to him with sliced-up feet.

"No, I don't think so." He hopped around. "Can you hurry? I really need to pee."

"Sorry." Inwardly, Rosie scolded herself. She really should have helped him to the bathroom before she'd fallen asleep. She skirted the bed and put her arm around his waist and felt only warm, male skin. She'd forgotten he was buck naked except for a robe. "Okay."

"You totally forgot I was naked except for a robe, didn't you?" He leaned on her as they shuffled to the bathroom.

"Yes." She would offer no further comment on his state of undress, and she tried really hard to keep her eyes looking forward instead of down. She'd put his clothes in the dryer hours ago. While he answered nature's call, she'd slip into the kitchen and pull them out of the dryer.

They shuffled into the bathroom, and she decided against turning on the light. It was enough that she felt the tapering-in of his hips and the rock-hard muscles of his back; she really didn't need to see him too. When they made it into the bathroom, she came up short.

"How do you want to do this?" She hoped he wouldn't go into detail, but she was willing to admit there were some logistical problems. He couldn't stand by himself to pee, plus the light was off, and she didn't want to think about the cleanup that might be involved with his seriously limited field of vision. Would he take it as a slight against his manhood if she suggested he sit down?

"I can practically hear the wheels turning in your head. Just help me sit down and I'll take care of the rest." His breath tickled her ear.

She opened the door to the closet-sized room that held the toilet and helped him down on the seat. She stepped out and closed the door. Liquid hit water as she made it to the kitchen. She folded back the accordion doors that hid the stacked washer and dryer. She hit start on the dryer just to freshen the clothes and pull out any wrinkles. Plus, warm clothes always felt good.

She went back to the bathroom, and liquid was still hitting water. Not wanting to interrupt him, she went back to the dryer and pulled his clothes out. For lack of anything better to do, she carefully folded his shirt, boxer-briefs, jeans, and socks. She grabbed the boxers and the shirt and left the remaining clothes on the sofa. She headed back to the bathroom.

The toilet flushed and then all she heard was silence.

She knocked on the door. "Are you finished? At the risk of sounding gross and unladylike, that was some championship peeing. Your bladder must be the size of Lake Michigan."

She wasn't trying to hurry him, but she wanted him to know she was ready to help.

"I'm done. Come in." There was a smile in his voice. "I have been blessed with an extra-large bladder."

She opened the door and found him already standing. She kept her eyes on his face. "I brought your clean boxers and shirt in case you'd like to put them on."

"Are you afraid you'll lose all control in the presence of my nearly naked self?" The grin in his voice turned cocky.

"I think I can control myself." She handed him the clothes.

"Warm clothes. Nice." He put his arm around her. "Can you help me back to bed and then back into my shorts?"

"Your wish is my command." She took his weight and they shuffled back to bed.

"Really? I can think of all sorts of wishes." His hip kept bumping hers. "Want to know what I'm wishing now?"

"Does it involve sleep?" She couldn't help but smile. Even in the middle of the night, as they were stranded for God only knew how long and he had a broken ankle, he was still a horny male. In her experience, sex took first, second, and third place in every man's life, leaving little room for beer and food—the other two things men cherished.

He leaned close to her ear. "Not at first. Don't get me wrong, I'm not opposed to sleep and I prefer it to most other activities, but what I have in mind requires mental acuity and dexterity and a love of pleasure."

"Let me guess, you're referring to sex." She couldn't help the eye roll. "At first, I thought you were talking about chess, but the pleasure part most certainly refers to sex."

"Only if you do it right." His voice was dark-chocolate covered sin. "Actually, I wasn't referring to sex, and I'll thank you to get your mind out of the gutter. I of course was talking about the pleasures of the midnight snack. Specifically, more ice cream."

"I don't think we have any ice cream left." She hadn't thoroughly inspected the freezer, but she was pretty sure there had only been the one carton. The Villa hadn't been fully stocked yet. "Wait, how do you need mental acuity and dexterity to eat ice cream?"

He leaned heavily on the bed and eased himself down. "You have to be able to read the label. Trust me, you don't want to eat expired ice cream. I'm speaking from experience here. When the ice cream tastes funny, throw it away."

"And the dexterity?" How exactly was she supposed to help him on with his boxers?

"Only the highest-functioning mammals have opposable thumbs. You can't pop the lid on a pint of Blue Bell Home-made Vanilla without opposable thumbs. And sometimes even with opposable thumbs there's some weird suction thing going on and it takes brute strength to pry that lid off. Think about it. If dogs could open a pint, there'd be tons of meat-flavored ice creams. I, for one, am grateful that God chose to bestow only humans with the highest evolutionary honor." He exercised his opposable thumbs in front of her face to prove his point.

"What about the other primates? They have opposable thumbs too." She loved how his mind worked. It was so bizarre yet charming.

"Yeah, but they don't have money, and I'm not sure they could fully appreciate mint chocolate chip. Their palate isn't sophisticated enough to detect the fudge flakes in Cherry Garcia." He sounded like it was the sanest argument in the world.

"What about Chunky Monkey? I bet they can appreciate Chunky Monkey." She knelt down in front of him and gently worked his feet through the leg holes of the boxers. She made it all the way to his knee before he put a hand on her shoulder.

Now that her eyes had adjusted to the darkness, it was really hard not to notice everything about him, what with him sprawled out on the bed in front of her. She should stand and look away, only her body wasn't listening to her mind.

"I can take it from here." He lay down, inched the shorts

up his thighs, and up over his hips. "Stop licking my body with your eyes. I'm not just a piece of meat. I have feelings and ideas. There's more to me than just a hot body." There was a whole lot of mock outrage.

"Sorry, I was just..." She stood and turned her back to him. Her whole body felt flushed, and not in a good way.

"Ah ha. You were checking me out." His ego practically sucked all of the air out of the room. "I knew it. You know, you could take off your clothes and let me check you out. That way we'd be even." He made it sound like he was doing this solely for her benefit.

"You'd do that for me?" She made her voice go all high and squeaky. "That is so helpful." She paused for dramatic effect. "Thanks, but I'm good."

"Well... later, if you get to feeling guilty, the offer still stands." He made it sound like his generous spirit knew no boundaries. "Now, about that ice cream."

"I'm pretty sure we don't have any more, and even if we do, I'm not sure you'd want to eat it. I don't think the generator stays on at night." At least that's how she thought the generator worked.

"Did you have to turn it on when you first got here?" He push-dragged himself into an upright position against the headboard.

"No." Come to think of it, it was a propane generator, and she had no idea how they got propane to it. She really felt like she should know these things, but tech stuff wasn't her strong suit.

"The generator stays on all the time because my mother insisted on that. The propane line runs directly to the generator. We couldn't get electricity out here because we'd have to install seven poles and two transformers, but there's a propane hub for this side of the ranch about a quarter of a mile north." He certainly knew his stuff.

"I vaguely remember something about a propane line. Wasn't it back in January? I think I was working on the Boots and Black Tie Inaugural Ball." She really should have been more involved. Usually, micromanaging was her middle name. She hated that something as big as this had got by her. "I should have been more on top of things."

"Why? We had it handled." He chuckled. "You can't stand that there are details you don't know about your B&B. Hello, control freak."

"I'm not a control freak, I just like to be…" She was about to say "in control." Why was she denying her inner control freak? She knew she was one, and so did everyone else. She needed to let her control-freak flag fly.

"Let me guess, this is the first time you've ever really relinquished some of the control?" He didn't sound judgmental. It was just an observation.

"Yes." She still couldn't wrap her head around it. "What else have I missed?"

"You didn't miss anything, you just let others step in and take some of the burden for once. You don't have to do everything yourself. I choose to think of it as you trusting us all enough to let us help out." He reached out and took her hand. "That's a good thing. And you obviously didn't worry about it because you knew we could handle it."

She hadn't thought of that. Maybe there was help for her inner control freak; then again, she liked being in control, which meant she liked controlling her inner control freak. It was a vicious cycle.

He squeezed her hand and let go. "Now, why don't you check the freezer."

"Okay." She stopped herself from saying, "Your wish is

my command," because that was how this whole conversation had started in the first place.

She opened the freezer side of the side-by-side refrigerator, and sure enough, down at the bottom were two entire rows filled with pints of ice cream. There was quite a mixture of Blue Bell, Ben & Jerry's, and Häagen-Dazs. The other shelves held white-butcher-paper-wrapped bundles of meat.

"What's your poison?" Whoever had stocked the freezer was fast becoming her most favorite person.

"Anything with lots of chocolate will do," he called from the bedroom.

She grabbed a pint of Häagen-Dazs Chocolate Chocolate Chip and two spoons and turned toward the bedroom.

If the freezer was this well stocked, what was in the fridge?

She paused to open the fridge. There were several kinds of cheese, five bottles of white wine, a case of Shiner beer, a case of bottled water, and a bottle of ketchup, and that was just on the first shelf. The other shelves were packed too. Wow, she really had trusted others a lot.

For her, that was monumental. The best part was that she was okay with doing it again.

14

Dallas sent up a silent prayer of thanks at his good fortune. He moved his left leg and winced at the pain. Okay, so the ankle was bad news, but being stranded with Rosie was good news.

If he'd planned this stranding, it couldn't have gone better. Well, okay, again the ankle, but still. Things were coming together nicely.

Rosie was hot, funny, into sci-fi, and she was opening up to him. This was definitely a step in the right direction.

She walked into the bedroom carrying a pint of ice cream and two spoons. "I can't believe I didn't check the fridge before. We're going to be eating well."

God bless his mother and her overpreparedness. And her love of ice cream. "If you find a bag of Jalapeño Cheetos, I call dibs." He glanced at the ice cream. "Häagen-Dazs Chocolate Chocolate Chip. It looks like my mother stocked the food. There will definitely be a hidden bag of Jalapeño Cheetos."

"I never noticed what a junk-foodie she is." Rosie

crawled onto the bed and handed him a spoon. "I really like that about her."

"Yeah, Mom's always been somewhat of a junk-food hypocrite. She'd wouldn't let us eat ice cream for dinner, but she sure would. My dad used to get onto her, but then she introduced him to Jalapeño Cheetos and he went over to the dark side. He's not much for ice cream, but cookies... he can put a serious dent in some chocolate chip cookies."

She worked the lid off the pint and pulled off the thin white piece of plastic covering the ice cream. She held the carton out for him to take the first bite.

He shook his head. "Ladies first."

She grinned. "I like your manners. I should give your mother a hug for doing such a good job."

"What about me?" He held his arms out. "Don't I deserve a hug?"

"You're kinda needy, aren't you?" She swirled her spoon in the ice cream and slowly brought it to her mouth.

He dropped his arms.

"You're just now noticing that? That's got to be a personal record for me." He glanced at the pale light sneaking behind the blinds. The sun was coming up, and it appeared that the rain had stopped.

"No, I'm just now mentioning it. I noticed it a while ago." She waited for him to take a bite, and then she swirled her spoon in the ice cream again and brought it to her lips.

"Thank God. It's important for me to get the word out that I'm high maintenance. The more people that know the better. That way people don't assume I'm easygoing. I find it saves time." He scooped up a bite and shoveled it in.

"I admire a man with a plan." She swirled and licked.

He'd never known that eating ice cream could be such a sensual experience, but watching her was absolutely turning him on. Then again, Rosie could rev his engine just by entering the room.

"Why are you staring at me?" She swirled and licked again.

He lowered his eyes. "Sorry, I didn't mean to stare."

"It's the ice cream. I eat it slowly. My sisters hate when I eat ice cream in front of them because it takes me forever. There is always at least one comment on how the ice cream will probably melt before I finish." If anything, she slowed down her swirl and lick.

"You savor it. I get that." His eyes locked on her spoon. "For what it's worth, they're wrong. Watching you eat ice cream is a religious experience."

"What's your favorite ice cream?" She continued at her own pace. Swirl and lick.

He thought about it for a couple of beats. "I don't discriminate. I like all ice cream." He held up a hand. "That's not true. I like normal ice cream flavors. When you start making ice cream out of corn on the cob or red-eye gravy, it's just nasty. Savory ice cream is a terrible idea. Once, on the Food Network, someone made pimento cheese ice cream. Why would anyone make that, and more importantly, why would they think anyone would want to eat it?"

She shrugged. "I'm with you. I don't want to eat the flavors of Thanksgiving—i.e., the turkey and dressing—made into ice cream. I saw that once on the Food Network. Why would anyone ruin a perfectly good roasted turkey and perfectly good cream to make something so disgusting?"

"You got me." He scooped up another bite. "Some things I just don't understand."

Rosie glanced at the window. "Looks like the sun's coming up."

She went to the window and pulled on the cord, raising the blinds. "It's stopped raining."

The sun was bright and clear in the light-blue, cloudless sky.

She put her ear to the window like she was trying to hear the sunshine.

"What are you listening for?" He heard the faint sound of rushing water, but nothing else.

"The crowing rooster. I'm never up this early unless it's because I haven't gone to bed yet." She pressed her ear against the glass. "CanDee and Justus have remarked on many occasions that at least once in my life, I should hear the rooster crow."

"I take it you're not a morning person." He knew she wasn't, but he liked making conversation with her.

"Nope, and I don't apologize for it. Everyone has a vice and mine is sleeping late. I hate cheerful morning people." She turned around and leaned against the window. "Why do I get the feeling that you're one of those cheerful morning people?"

"I'm pretty sure that no one has ever called me cheerful unless they were drunk or I was drunk and misheard them." He spooned up another bite. "But I do like to start off the day with a big, healthy smile. Give me a quiet morning over a late night any day."

"Just when I was starting to like you." She shook her head. "I find out your dirty little secret. I don't think we can be friends anymore."

"What if I promise to be crabby and hateful until noon?" He loved just hanging out with her. There was no telling what would come out of her mouth next.

"It's a start, but it's not enough. I need for you to state all of your good qualities." She crossed her arms. "I warn you now, it better be a long and impressive list."

He laced his fingers behind his head. "Well now, let me see."

He put his right index finger against his pursed lips. "In the fourth grade, I won the Kendall County Spelling Bee for spelling the word 'milieu.' The next year, I distinctly remember letting Worth have my Rice Krispy Treat at lunch, but I guess that really doesn't count since I'd stolen it from him in the first place." He searched his brain. "In middle school, I helped a little old man cross the street, only it turns out he was a little old lady and she didn't want to cross the street. Then there was the time I saved a little lab-created mutant girl from the men that wanted to kill her and helped her get to Canada so she could live with other lab-created mutant children." He shook his head. "Wait... no, that was the movie *Logan*." He made a big show of thinking really hard. "I'm pretty sure I have some good qualities, but it appears that they're buried really deep."

"I see." She pursed her lips. "Maybe I can help. What do the Borg, the Peacekeepers, and the Alliance all have in common?"

"They're all bad guys, except for Seven of Nine and Aeryn Sun, who both started as bad guys but had a change of heart and started working for the good guys." Any half-way-decent sci-fi fan would know that.

"And just like that, you're back in my good graces." She turned back to the window and then froze.

"What's wrong?" Without thinking, he moved his leg and pain radiated out from his ankle.

She pointed to the glass. "I think I just saw several trees and a tractor float by."

He inched his way to the edge of the bed and held out his arm. "Help me up and let's go check on the river."

She wrapped her arm around him and shouldered his weight as he stood. They hobbled to the front door. She opened the door and they hobbled onto the front porch.

The sound of rushing water vibrated through the clear morning. The Villa was high enough and far enough back on a limestone shelf that they couldn't see the water, but they could hear it and see the tops of trees and debris as they floated by.

Rosie helped him to one of the rocking chairs and then took off in a dead run. She was in her bare feet, but she didn't seem to have noticed.

"Wait, don't get too close to the edge." He fisted his hands in frustration. What if she fell into the rushing water? There was nothing he could do but watch.

"I don't see my car. Where's my car?"

The panic in her voice tore at him.

She moved closer toward the running water. "Oh my God."

He shot out of the chair. Pain sliced through his body and his leg crumbled beneath him.

"Rosie, wait." He dragged himself to the edge of the porch.

She turned around. Her eyes were huge as she ran back toward him.

"What are you doing?" Dismay filled her voice. Her arms slid under his shoulders and she pulled him back to the rocking chair.

"I was trying to get to you. I thought something was wrong." He sucked in short gasps of air. The pain was making him nauseated.

Her eyes caught on something on the side of the Villa. "Stay here. I'll be right back."

She ran around the side of the house and came back pushing a wheelbarrow.

What exactly was she planning to do with that?

"Have a sudden urge to garden?" He gritted his teeth. If his ankle wasn't broken before, it sure was now.

"I'm going to use it to show you the river." She parked it on the crushed-granite path next to the five steps leading down to the yard.

He looked at the wheelbarrow, looked at Rosie, then looked back at the wheelbarrow. "Have you ever pushed someone around in one of those things? I don't know if you noticed while you were ogling me, but I'm not a small man. You're not even wearing shoes." He eyed her bare feet with skepticism. Her sexy toes would look a lot less sexy crushed by a wheelbarrow.

"How hard can it be?" She gave him an encouraging nod. "We're not going far, and I'll stay on level terrain."

He thought about it. "I guess the worst that could happen is I break my other ankle. What the heck, you only live once, right?" It wasn't every day a man got to witness a flood of biblical magnitude with a woman like Rosie by his side.

"Don't worry. I'll take good care of you." Ignoring his hesitation, she wrapped her arm around his waist and helped him down the steps and into the wheelbarrow.

"Ready?" She took a deep breath and hoisted up the wheelbarrow. "You're heavier than you look."

"Thanks, I'll take that as a compliment." He looked down at his ankle. It was black and blue and swelling around the duct tape.

She wheeled him along the gravel path toward the river. As they wheeled closer to the cliff, the roaring got louder.

When he caught site of the devastation, he forgot all about his ankle.

The Guadalupe River had been transformed from its normal calm, slow, tube-ride pace into a raging, angry beast. The churned-up chocolate-milk-colored water was still rising. He estimated it was advancing by at least an inch a minute. It was a good twenty-five feet below them, but they would need to keep an eye on it. Whole uprooted trees and large chunks of concrete rushed past them. A red pickup bobbed up and down as it passed by. And then there were the animals. Cows, pigs, and what looked like a deer all floated downriver, their lifeless bodies a true testament to just how devastating Mother Nature could be.

Thank God Rosie had taken shelter when she did. His heart was in his throat just thinking about what could have happened to her.

"There's nothing left." Rosie pointed to the bank that had once housed luxury teepees and even more luxurious cabins. "They're gone."

His family had to be safe. They knew to go to higher ground. He glanced upriver, looking for the hundred-year-old cypress tree that had held the zip line. Either he was too far away from it or it was gone because the river had swallowed everything on its banks.

"What are we going to do?" She glanced down at him and then to his ankle. "I'm so sorry. You're in pain and I'm whining about my business."

She pushed him back to the cabin and helped him up the stairs and back to bed.

"Let me get you some ice and some ibuprofen." She went to the kitchen and he heard her opening the fridge and freezer and putting ice into a bag. She returned with a glass of milk and a towel-wrapped bundle of ice, which she gently laid on his foot. She upended the ibuprofen bottle she'd left on the nightstand and shook out five tablets. She handed them to him along with the glass of milk.

He downed the pills, and the ice was starting to numb some of the pain.

"I hate to ask you to do anything else for me, but could you use the sat phone to call my parents? You could try the Lodge if they're not home. We were using the Lodge as a headquarters to look for you."

"Oh my God, I'm so sorry. I should have done that as soon as I saw the river." She ran into the living room and then he heard the front door slam.

He heard her voice but he couldn't make out the words.

God, please let his family be okay. They got on his nerves and were sometimes a pain in the ass, but his life didn't work without them.

Someone tapped on the window next to the bed, and he jumped about a foot in the air. His eyes went to the window.

Rosie waved. "Unlock it." Her voice was muffled.

He reached over and flipped the metal toggle that unlocked the window. She pushed it up.

"I'm going to put you on speaker—that is, if I can figure out how to put you on speaker." She pushed a couple of buttons.

"How's his ankle?" His father's voice boomed out from the speakerphone.

"It's pretty black and blue and swollen. He just tried to walk on it and reinjured it." Rosie eyed him like he was in trouble for that. "Tell him that he needs to keep off of it."

"Dallas, stay in bed. I know it's not in your nature to

listen to me, but this time you will. Stay off that ankle." His father was using his you'd-better-listen-to-me-or-else voice.

Dallas wasn't promising anything. "Is everyone okay?"

"Promise me you'll stay off that ankle. Your mother made me promise I'd tell you before she went to the hospital several hours ago. And you know I hate to upset your mother." His father knew him too well.

"Okay, I promise. Now, is everyone all right?" His voice was high and squeaky but he didn't care. This was his family and he couldn't lose any of them.

"Yes, everyone here is safe. The river is rising rapidly and the news says that the water won't crest for another day or so. I'm afraid we can't get to you until then. All of the bridges are washed out, and all search-and-rescue personnel are actively searching for the missing." His father's voice caught. "There's a whole family who were in a cabin upstream that washed away. It's a mess." He could hear the sorrow in his father's voice. His dad was big and strong and had a soft spot for any and everyone. "I've got the grandkids with me. Everyone else has gone into Roseville to help out in any way they can. Some of the displaced families are on the way here. We're going to put them up until things are sorted out."

"Feel free to put some people in my house." Dallas had seen the river but he couldn't fathom the destruction. It would take years to overcome one night's heavy rain.

"And the cottage. Please feel free to offer them my clothes or toiletries or whatever I have that may be need-ed." Rosie fisted her hands, and Dallas could feel the frus-tration rolling off of her. "I wish I was there to help." She snapped her fingers. "Oh, yesterday morning I got a huge shipment of T-shirts and robes in for the B&B. There are also the toiletries and linens that came in last week.

They're all in the cottage's living room. Y'all could hand them out."

"That's very thoughtful of you. I'll make sure we get the supplies." Someone mumbled something in the background. "Rosie, Hugh would like to speak with you."

There was some shifting on the phone.

"Hey, Rosie. Louisa just called again to make sure you were okay. I told her that you and Dallas were safe and in a house, but that you were on the other side of the river. All your sisters were so worried that they're on their way to Roseville and guess what?" Hugh's voice held nothing but his excitement for adventure. He was too young to appreciate what had been lost.

Rosie smiled. "What, Big H?"

"They're bringing the Flan truck. They're going to park outside of Roseville High School where people are meeting who need help and they're going to give out free flan." He made it sound so exciting.

Dallas could relate. Free flan was pretty damn exciting.

"That sounds like fun." Rosie loved Hugh, and it was clear from the way her whole body smiled.

"I know. Louisa promised me I could help hand out the flan." Hugh sounded very proud of his important new responsibility. "Guess what else?"

"What?"

"Your sisters called some other people they know and there's like ten food trucks coming. They're all going to hand out free food." Hugh sounded just like he had on Christmas morning.

"I wish we could be there," Dallas said.

"Me too," Rosie added.

There was some more mumbling on Hugh's side of the phone.

"Oh, I gotta go. Mary's taking me to town so I can help out. Bear's gonna stay here in case y'all need anything and to watch AG." There was some shuffling like someone had picked up the phone. "Just so you know, I watched over AG all night last night cause I'm her big brother. I kept her safe from the thunder just like you told me, Uncle Dallas." Hugh was all self-importance.

"Good job, H-man. I knew you were big brother material." Dallas loved that boy to death.

"Okay, I gotta go." The phone line went dead.

"In the mind of a little boy, there's nothing more important than free food." Rosie laughed as she closed the window.

It occurred to Dallas that he didn't know Rosie's stance on kids. He knew she loved Hugh, but did she want any of her own?

Someday he hoped to have a boy just like Hugh.

If Dallas had his way, it would be sooner rather than later.

15

"Sorry you have to miss the free flan." Rosie stood over a hot cast-iron skillet. She smiled to herself. It had been hours since they'd spoken with Hugh, and she had this image of him handing out flan to people whether they wanted it or not.

"Since I now have an 'in' with Fantastic Flans, I plan on eating lots of free flan." Dallas was lying back on the sofa while she cooked dinner.

He was getting a little stir-crazy in the bed, so she'd moved him into the living room for a change of scenery. They'd been making periodic phone calls to the Lodge for updates. There were still twenty people missing, including nine members—three generations—of the same family.

Rosie felt guilty for even thinking of her car, but she had a bad feeling it was long gone.

She salted and peppered the two filets mignons she'd defrosted and laid them in the hot cast-iron pan. They sizzled beautifully.

"So, any idea what happened to my car?" She turned around and knew she looked sheepish but she couldn't help it. "I know there are worse things going on, but Rhonda was my first adult purchase."

"Her name was Rhonda?" He adjusted the pillow behind his head.

"Was?" She opened a can of green beans and poured it into a pot. She turned the nob on the stove and the flame caught under the pan.

"Yeah, I have some bad news. Rhonda didn't make it." He held up a hand. "But she did sacrifice her life for you."

"I don't understand." She added salt and pepper to the beans. She really didn't have much in the way of spices to make the canned beans edible.

"Well, it's kind of complicated." He scratched the back of his neck and avoided her eyes.

"Okay, I'm listening." Was it just her or was he purposely being evasive?

"Rhonda went swimming. Some of the ranch hands saw her floating down the river. We didn't know if you were inside when she took her swim." He still wouldn't make eye contact. "She was upside down."

"Upside down?" How was that possible?

"Your Rover had flipped over and the tires were up. We thought you were inside and..." The word "dead" hung in the air.

She flipped the steaks. "Okay, I understand my Rover being upside down. Is that why you came looking for me?"

If he thought she was dead, then why risk his life looking for her?

"Yes. I needed to find you and make sure you were okay." He kept his eyes down.

"Why? I mean, why not just leave it to the profession-als?" He could have waited and let the first responders locate her. He didn't need to risk his life for someone who everyone thought was dead anyway.

Was it possible he cared about her too much to wait? She felt a tingle right around her heart.

He finally looked up and stared her dead in the eyes. "I have more than just a big crush on you. I had to make sure you were safe because I care about you."

The tingle turned into a full-blown glow.

She turned the heat off of the cooking food, slid a spatula under the steaks, and set them on a plate to rest.

She went to him. "I don't know if I said thank you, but thank you." She kissed him on the cheek. "I needed to get that out of the way before I did this..."

She swung a leg over his torso, straddled him, and lowered herself onto his lap.

The look of shock on his face was priceless.

"Just so you know," she said, "we're about to have sex, because I care about you too. I'm not doing this because I feel that I owe you anything. It's important that you know that." She whipped off her red T-shirt and kissed him for all she was worth.

His hands went to her back, pulling her down on top of him. "Just so you know, because I have a crush on you, I totally would have taken the pity sex. I'm man enough to admit that."

"God, you're cute." She kissed him hard.

"I try." His hands found her breasts. "I like you braless. I've been looking for a politically correct way of saying that all day."

Her hands slid down his hard chest. "Funny, I've been trying to find a way to compliment you on your nice body. It's harder than you think."

"Not to put a damper on things, but I think the bed

would be a better place for this." He rocked back and forth. The dainty Queen Anne sofa creaked and groaned. "I don't think this sofa can take it. Plus my range of motion is too limited. I want to make a good impression, and for that I need a sturdier piece of furniture."

"Then let's get you to bed." She slid off him and circled his waist with her arm, helping him up. Their normal slow shuffle morphed into a super-fast-forward shuffle. She helped him onto the bed, and he lay back against the pillows.

He tried to pull her down on top of him, but she wiggled out of his grasp. She stood next to the bed, tucked her thumbs into the waistband of the yoga pants, and slowly shimmied out of them.

"Wow." His eyes raked down her body. "You are the most beautiful thing I have ever seen."

She suppressed the urge to roll her eyes. In her experience, men would say just about anything to get laid.

He whistled as his eyes lingered on the cleft between her legs. "Miss Gomez, I believe you are missing some serious undergarments." He nodded his approval. "You are really fucking naked. Wow."

She leaned forward and her hands went to his boxers.

He lifted his hips and she pulled the boxers down his legs and gently worked them over his feet.

He was beautifully made. She let her eyes have free rein over the peaks and valleys of his stomach. They dipped lower and she mashed her lips together to keep from whistling her own approval. He was hard and ready.

"Being a responsible man, I feel that I should point out that we don't have any condoms." His eyes fixed onto her breasts.

She leaned over, picked up the backpack, and pulled out

box. "I'm guessing it was Justus who packed the bag. She sent a box of twelve."

He held out his hand, and she gave him the box. He had it opened and was rolling one down his shaft before she had time to climb into the bed.

She lay down next to him and ran her index finger up and down his chest. "I like your chest."

He grinned like a fool. "Back at you Rosie Posy."

"Rosie Posy?" She kissed his jaw and licked her way down to his left pec.

"The name I've called you in my head since the first day I saw you." His muscles quivered under her tongue. He put a hand on her chin and tilted it up so she could meet his eyes. "It looks like you're having all of the fun. Come back up here and kiss me."

She licked her way back up his chest and laid her lips on his. His tongue darted playfully into her mouth as he shifted her so that she was straddling his good leg. He leaned forward, placing his hands on her thighs and sliding them up to rest on her ass.

He broke the kiss and his mouth found her left nipple. He licked and sucked.

He sat back and licked his lips. "Since my mobility is seriously limited, I'm going to need a little help."

She placed a hand on the pillows on either side of his head and smiled down into his eyes. "Name it."

"Could you inch a little bit farther up?" His hands went to her ass and gently urged her forward.

"Like this?" She worked her way up and stopped at the juncture of his thighs. She shifted, teasing his groin.

"That's... really... *really* nice. But I need you to move a little bit farther up." He urged her upward with the pressure of his hands.

She worked her way up and up until her core was inches from his mouth. "Like this?"

"Just a little bit more." His hands moved to the front of her thighs and spread her legs even wider. He licked the inside of her thighs as his finger found her clit. He stroked and licked. She leaned forward, grabbing the wrought-iron headboard with one hand and tunneling her fingers through his hair with the other.

His mouth found her clit while a finger dipped inside her. Her body found his rhythm and warm heat tingled through her system, building to something more. Her hips urged him to move faster and faster and faster. Twinges of scorching pleasure burned through her. She urged him to move faster. The orgasm crashed through her and she arched her back, wanting to prolong it for as long as she could.

As heat streaked through her, her head fell back.

His hands circled her hips and moved her down his torso and settled her firmly on his cock.

This wasn't right. She wanted to return the favor. "Wait, it's your turn to—"

She made to climb off, but his hands clamped down, holding her firmly in place.

"Here's the thing..." His breathing was labored. With his hands, he lifted her hips and then urged them down. "I've been fantasizing about this... pretty much... since the moment I laid eyes on you..." He bit his lower lip and his eyes closed as he moved her up and down. She caught on to his rhythm with her hips, and his hands found her breasts.

"How's reality holding up against your fantasy?" Slowly, she sat up and then back down. Up and down. Up and down.

"You are better than I could have ever imagined." His

hands returned to her hips to try to increase the rhythm, but she was having none of that.

She had power over him, and that was the best aphrodisiac.

Sitting back on her knees, she took her time riding him.

His left hand moved from her breasts to her back, pushing her forward so that her breasts were close to his mouth. He licked and sucked one nipple and then the other while his right hand clamped down hard on her hip, insisting she increase their rhythm.

She relented and followed his lead. The harder she rode him, the more he seemed to want it. He took her nipple fully in his mouth as she drove them both closer and closer to climax. The orgasm exploded through her body, and she felt his pleasure overtake him too. She pumped her hips until the very end, and then she rolled off of him, sated and spent.

"That was amazing." She was breathing hard and she'd worked up quite a sweat.

"Wow." He wrapped his arm around her and pulled her in close to nuzzle his chest. His breathing was hard. "'Wow' really doesn't do it justice, but my brain is broken and that's the only word that comes to mind."

Speaking of broken body parts... she glanced down at his ankle. "That was pretty athletic. Is your ankle okay?" She inspected the injury. It didn't look any worse than it already had.

"Ankle? I have ankles? What ankle?" His breathing was slowly returning to normal.

"I'll take that as a compliment." She laid her head on his chest. "I know it's too soon, but can we do that again? I feel like we have eleven more condoms to go. I hate to be wasteful."

"I admire your thrifty nature." He smacked her on the ass. "I plan on using every single one of those condoms.

"Good." She liked snuggling with Dallas, and more importantly, she liked him as a person. She could get used to this. She could get used to having him in her life.

16

Dallas was pretty sure that his life had turned perfect. He couldn't help the smile. In fact, he'd probably be smiling like an idiot for the rest of his life.

Rosie was everything he wanted and more... so much more.

Right now, she was in the kitchen wearing nothing but his shirt and finishing the steaks that she'd started an hour ago. While they ate, they were going to watch the first season of *Farscape*.

Sex, steak, and a sci-fi marathon. What more could a man ask for?

The world around them was washing away. People had been hurt, lives and property had been lost, but here in their little bubble, life was wonderful.

He wanted to tell Rosie that he loved her, but it was too soon.

Was it really though?

Didn't women want to hear "I love you"? Plenty of

women had told him that they loved him and had cried when he hadn't said the words back. Now he was on the other end of the situation—what if Rosie didn't say it back?

Yep, it was too early to tell her. Besides his mother, he'd never said those three little words to a woman. Now that he thought about it, he'd never said that phrase to anyone outside of his family. And he could probably count on one hand the number of times he'd said it to them.

He was definitely not an "I love you" slut. Maybe he should make that clear to Rosie before he told her. Otherwise, she might think he used the words "I love you" like hipsters used the word "like."

How exactly was he supposed to show her that he didn't take those three little words lightly?

Love was turning out to be way more complicated than he'd thought.

Talking to women had never been his problem. Worth, on the other hand, overthought everything, which led to shyness. Dallas was the verbal twin, while Worth was the mechanical twin. That had always been their roles, at least until Rosie had come along and turned Worth into a silver-tongued devil.

She walked into the bedroom with a plate and silverware in each hand. She set the plates down on the nightstand. "I'll get the wine."

"Wine?" He could stand to spend the next million nights just like this one. "I thought there was only white wine in the fridge."

She walked back in holding two wine glasses in one hand and a bottle of Rowdy's Rustic Sauvignon Blanc in the other. "Don't tell Rowdy that we're having white wine with red meat. I'm not sure he could take that news."

"I never discuss wine with my older brother. He throws

out terms no regular person would know, which makes me feel inferior, which makes me angry, which makes me deck him." Everyone in the family knew not to discuss wine with Rowdy. It wasn't worth the hassle.

"You and all of your brothers punch each other a lot." She set the glasses next to the plates and poured the wine.

"It's how we communicate. I like to think of it as a love beatdown." Crap, now she'd think that he punched everyone he loved. "I don't punch everyone I love, only my brothers."

He reviewed that last sentence in his mind. Yep, it made sense.

"My sisters and I don't punch each other, but we do argue loudly." She laughed. "The first time Hugh came over for dinner with my family, he put his hands over his ears because we were all being so loud."

"The Rose clan has been known to get a little boisterous at times." He watched her walk over to the other side of the bed.

He handed her a plate and one set of silverware and then took the other plate and set it in his lap. "Do you want me to keep your wine on the nightstand, or do you want to balance it in your lap?"

"On the nightstand is fine." She glanced at the empty space next to her side of the bed. "I thought two nightstands was one nightstand too much, but I can see that we really need two in here."

It sounded like she was taking mental notes.

"Then it's good that we're testing the room out before the B&B goes live." Right after the words left his mouth, he wanted to thunk himself on the forehead. This was the only room left of her B&B.

"Well, now we have lots of time to test things out." She

sighed long and hard. "I'm choosing to see this as an opportunity to fix all of the things we did wrong."

"Like what?" He couldn't imagine that there was much that Rosie did wrong. She didn't need do-overs because she planned everything to within an inch of its life.

"No idea. We didn't get far enough into things to have problems." She cut a dainty bite of steak and brought it to her mouth.

"Sorry about your B&B." He watched her carefully. He could see that she was retreating inward. It seemed that in times of crisis, she looked inward. Or maybe she just wanted to hide from the pain of it. He hadn't meant to make her sad. "Let's talk about something else. Hugh was so excited to be handing out flan."

A wide smile spread across her face. "I love that kid. He used to come and stay with us when Justus was out of town and her father and stepmother were also out of town. We never had a little brother, so my sisters and I didn't know what to expect. He charmed every one of us into doing whatever he wanted."

"Four women to wait on him hand and foot. Every man's dream."

Rosie punched him playfully in the arm. "Justus always said that it took a good two weeks to beat the Gomez out of him because we spoiled him so much." She shot Dallas an I'm-sorry look. "Without a doubt, Hugh's my most favorite male in the whole wide world."

"Hey now, I'm pretty awesome." He tried not to sound like a whiny baby, but Hugh was moving in on his girl. To be fair, Hugh had been there first, but still.

"Again with the needy." She stabbed a green bean and popped it in her mouth. Her face blanched and it seemed all she could do not to spit it out. She chewed and chewed and finally swallowed it. "Sorry, those are terrible. I didn't have much to work with."

Based on her reaction, he was steering clear of the green beans. He cut into his steak. It was a perfect medium rare. He tasted it. It just about melted on his tongue. "This is wonderful."

"Thank you. It is pretty good, if I do say so myself." She popped in another bite.

"So tell me more about yourself." He felt like when it came to her interests and her life, he'd only touched the tip of the iceberg.

She swallowed the bite in her mouth. "What do you want to know?"

"Everything. Start at the beginning." He was ready to jump in to their life together.

"I'm going to need wine." She pointed to her wineglass.

He handed it to her.

"There's really not much. My childhood left a lot to be desired—you know that part. My mother died, and my much-older sisters took me in." She downed half of the wine. "I started planning events in college. It turns out that I was really good at it. After graduation, I went into business as an event planner. At the end of my first year, I got the opportunity to plan a huge, high-profile wedding. After that, it was weddings all the time." She sipped her wine. It didn't go unnoticed that she gulped while talking about her childhood but only sipped when talking about life after childhood. She'd told him everything about her mother, and the woman had sounded pretty awful, but clearly it still hurt her to talk about her childhood. "That's not strictly true. I did a few other events, but mainly I planned weddings." She smiled. "For the most part, I enjoyed it."

"Why give it up?" Not that he wanted her to return to

wedding planning, since it would mean her leaving the ranch.

"It's time. I've enjoyed it, but it's time for a new challenge. Planning a wedding at Burning Man with absolutely no amenities, and now finishing my career with the wedding of the year for one of my best friends—I couldn't ask for a better ending." She was completely sincere.

"No regrets?" He just wanted to make sure. He would hate for her to leave a career that she loved.

She shook her head. "None. I would regret it if I didn't try the B&B. It was my idea. I'm excited at the prospect of starting something new." She rolled her eyes. "I was, I mean. And I guess I still am." She opened her mouth to say more and then closed it.

"What?" He never wanted to leave things unsaid.

"I don't... I mean, I feel..." She blew a stray lock of hair out of her eyes. "I feel like a whiny little baby because I'm upset about losing the B&B. In light of all of the devastation, I feel horrible that I'm sad about something that isn't that important."

"It's important to you. It's okay for you to feel a loss." He'd never seen the vulnerable side of Rosie. She seemed softer, and it only made her more loveable.

"So many people have lost family members, not to mention their homes. It feels self-centered to mourn the loss of my business." She held up a hand. "Rephrase. The temporary loss of my business. We're insured and we'll build again." She gritted her teeth and shook her head. "It just feels petty."

She handed him her wineglass, and he set it on the nightstand.

"It's your turn. Tell me about you." She popped another steak bite into her mouth.

"Not much to tell." Compared to her, there really wasn't much to tell. "Average childhood. Came home after college and started working for the family business." He thought about it for a second. "I just noticed that I'm pretty boring."

"Come on. There's more to you than just that." She folded her legs under her and turned inquisitive eyes on him. "You run the hunting and game side of the business and the exotic-animal ranch. From what I hear, you've built up a revenue stream that didn't exist before. That's impressive."

"I guess. I've never really thought about it." He worked hard. She was right. He had built something from the ground up. "You've been checking up on me."

"I'm not going to lie. I might have done some research on you. Former volunteer firefighter and lover of animals... I might have seen a few articles online about you." She reached for her iPad on the bed and then changed her mind. "Ugh, no internet. If we had internet, I'd show you."

"You found articles about me?" Why in the hell would anyone write an article about him?

"What? You've never googled yourself?" She reached for her iPad again and then stopped herself. "I seem to be going through internet withdrawal. I've never really thought of myself as tech obsessed, but here I am whining about the internet."

He covered her hand with his, brought her hand to his lips, and kissed her palm. "We're a product of our environment. We can't help but be dependent on the internet. What must it have been like before the internet? Back in the dinosaur age, when people had cellphones that only called other people." He shook his head. "That's just craziness right there."

"I know. I vaguely remember life before high-speed

internet. I think we had to use a modem—you know, that thing that calls the internet." She set her fork and knife on her plate and placed it next to her. "Just think, in the future our children will sit and wonder how we made it through life with lowly old smartphones."

He liked the sound of "our children."

"I can't even imagine what their world will be like." He set his plate on the nightstand and pointed to hers. "Are you finished?"

"Yes." She drew her knees to her chest. "Maybe all travel will be via transporter. It would be nice to hit a button and be able to have dinner in Paris and then be back at home, sleeping in my bed."

Did he get to come along? He'd be happy sleeping in her bed too.

She rested her chin on her knees. "Who knows? Maybe everything will be virtual by then. You won't have to leave your house to do anything. Just put on the VR glasses and go." She wrinkled her nose. "Call me old school, but VR doesn't interest me. Unless it's the holodeck like in *Star Trek*. At the touch of a button you could be back in the Roaring Twenties or become a rock-and-roll star. There's some appeal in that."

"So, you want to be a rock star?" He couldn't see it.

"No, thanks. I'm good. Fame has never appealed to me." She snuggled up against him. "How about you? Do you secretly want the whole world to know your name?"

"I don't know about people knowing my name, but I did have a brush with fame." It was as close to fame as he ever wanted to be.

"Really? What did you do?" She rested her arm on his chest.

"Remember that volunteer firefighter's job? We had a

calendar. I was Mr. July." He'd never felt more self-conscious than he had at that photo shoot. Well, until he'd met Rosie and lost his ability to form sentences.

"Really? I wonder how hard it will be to get my hands on a copy." She looked up at him through her lashes. "I will of course demand that you sign it."

"For you, I'll even include a personal inscription." He put his arm around her. "I might be able to fix you up with a copy. I hear my mother bought several hundred. I still don't know if she did it because she was proud or she just wanted to support the local volunteer fire department."

"Come on, she's the proudest mother I've ever met. Her family is the most important thing to her." Rosie played with a stray string on the comforter. "Why did you give up volunteer firefighting?"

"It turns out that the calendar worked a little too well. We made enough money to hire our first two full-time firefighters. The city kicked in some money and we got some state funding and now we have eleven full-time firefighters." He hunched a shoulder. "It's probably for the best. I was a terrible firefighter. Honestly, I did it for the girls."

"What girls?" She did that one-eyebrow-up thing.

"I know this is shocking, but there are some women who are turned on by a man in uniform." He didn't think that applied to Rosie, but if it did—who was he kidding, it probably did—he'd scrounge together a uniform and wear it every single day.

"Do volunteer firefighters have uniforms?" She snuggled into his arm and rested her head on his shoulder.

"Yes, matching windbreakers and baseball caps count as a uniform." Would he always be this happy just being with Rosie?

"That sounds like the neighborhood watch in the

building where we used to live." She laughed. "When I moved in with Louisa, I thought the people in the red windbreakers were a street gang. She pointed out that they were all over the age of seventy and carrying flashlights and not guns. She said that if they did start their own gang, they'd all break a hip while protecting their turf."

"Louisa sounds interesting." He couldn't wait to meet her and the rest of Rosie's sisters.

"She's intense. There's no denying that." Rosie's voice was neutral, so he couldn't tell if that was good or bad. "I owe them a lot."

"Why do you feel that you owe them?" He drew lazy circles on her upper back. She calmed him, and he hoped he did the same for her.

"They put their lives on hold to take care of me." She obviously loved her sisters. Why did she think she owed them? Family took care of family, at least they did in his world.

"Have they ever mentioned to you that you owe them?" He continued the lazy circles on her back.

"No, but I feel that I do. They kept me out of foster care."

"Have they ever made you feel that you owe them?" He hated to make her talk about something that upset her, but she needed to talk it out.

Not that Dallas was much of a talker-outer, but this was some heavy stuff she'd been dealing with, and he wanted to help her through it.

"No, I just know I do." She thought about it for a second. "Don't I? I guess they've never said anything about me owing them..."

She pursed her mouth, and he could tell she was doing some deep thinking.

"Suppose you had a little sister and she needed a place

to live and you took her in. Would she owe you?" He wanted to help her to see all sides of the situation.

"No. I would be happy to take her in. I never thought of it that way." She smiled. "I would have loved to have had a little sister."

"See, I don't think your sisters believe that you owe them." He kept on with the lazy circles on her back. She didn't seem to mind. "Does this have something to do with your mother?"

She stared off into space like she was sifting through memories. She took a deep breath and let it out slowly. "My mother used to look at me and say, 'What have you done today to justify living?' She always made me feel so small and useless."

"Christ. She was awful to you. No one deserves that." Too bad she was already dead. Was peeing on the woman's grave insult enough? He couldn't think of anything worse to do to her. "I don't suppose you'd tell me where she's buried."

"We had her cremated. She wanted her ashes scattered over Lake Travis." One side of Rosie's mouth turned up in a smile. "Louisa tied a rock to the urn and tossed it off Red Bud Isle in Lady Bird Lake instead. I don't know why."

He wasn't all that familiar with Austin, but he knew Red Bud Isle was where people's dogs went swimming. There were dogs peeing on that urn. "This might seem like a weird question, but how did your mother feel about dogs?"

"She completely loathed them." Rosie thought about it for a second before awareness kicked in. "Now I get why Louisa went out of her way not to respect my mother's wishes." She nodded against his shoulder. "Now that I look back on it, I love Louisa even more." She looked up at him. "Thanks for making me see that."

"You're welcome." He hoped this was just the first time of many that he would be able to comfort her.

17

Whoever it was who'd first said that all good things must come to an end had been wise beyond their years. Two days later, Worth, Rowdy, and Cinco crossed the Guadalupe in a Zodiac. Lucy had told Rosie on the sat phone that they were coming, but it had been surreal to see three familiar faces walking across the front yard.

Dallas's ankle was bad and he needed help, but Rosie had to admit that she'd liked spending alone time with him. With the arrival of his brothers, their little bubble of unreality had burst. It was back to normal.

She watched as Worth and Cinco carried Dallas down the porch and across the front yard.

Rosie wasn't sure that there was a normal anymore.

Surely Dallas wouldn't go back to not being able to talk to her.

Rowdy took her work tote from her and pointed to her Jimmy Choos. "Sorry, no shoes in the Zodiac."

He wiggled his bare feet to drive the point home.

"You're the first person I've ever seen who wore an

Armani suit to a boat rescue." She stepped out of her heels and picked them up.

"Been in lots of water rescues, have you?" He matched her pace as they walked across the front yard.

"You have a point." She shaded her eyes from the blazing sun. "How bad is the devastation now that the water's receded?"

They got to the edge of the limestone cliff, and her breath caught in her throat. Trees were upended everywhere, and a blue car of some unknown make was tangled in what had to be a hundred-foot-tall cypress tree. Chunks of concrete and broken boards dotted the mud-covered bank. Across the river, only the concrete pads of the cabins remained.

Rowdy put a hand on her shoulder. "I don't mean to minimize your loss of the B&B, but this is nothing. Most of downtown Roseville is gone. Five hundred houses were leveled and thousands of people are now homeless. We've got seven families staying with us."

"It's both horrible and amazing what a little water can do." She followed his lead down the little path that led to the swollen riverbank. She stumbled and Rowdy caught her before she fell.

"Get your hands off my woman," Dallas yelled from the boat. "What the hell are you even doing here?"

Cinco shrugged. "You got me." He pointed to Worth. "We did all the work."

"Excuse me, I'm carrying Rosie's bag, which is something I bet neither of you Neanderthals thought to do." Rowdy helped Rosie climb into the boat. "I'm also here for moral support." He clapped his hands and smiled overbrightly at Cinco and then Worth. "Good job, guys."

"Think Mom would notice if we threw him overboard

and held him down?" Cinco pulled the chain to start the outboard motor.

"Nah, but Justus is bound to miss him." Worth used a paddle to push away from shore. "Then again, we could make it look like an accident."

"Stop talking about killing me in front of Rosie. She won't know you're kidding." Rowdy handed her an orange life vest.

She shrugged it on and buckled it.

"Who says we're kidding?" Cinco steered the boat toward the opposite bank.

"How come I didn't get a life vest?" Dallas, who was lying down in the bow, pointed to the vest Rosie had just buckled on.

"It's simple." Worth knelt beside Dallas. "We don't like you."

"With all of the love I'm feeling in this boat, we don't need a motor. We could power it solely on goodwill." Dallas rolled his eyes.

"You sound like a hippy or a hipster; they're pretty much interchangeable." Cinco aimed the boat toward Lefty, who was standing on the riverbank waving a couple of orange flags like he was directing a plane on the tarmac.

"Why is Lefty waving those flags?" She'd never seen anyone wave anything with as much gusto and self-importance.

Worth waved to Lefty. "He wanted to come with us, but he doesn't like the water. He fell into the lake as a kid and couldn't swim. We gave him the very important job of waving us to the shore."

"Why would he need to wave us to the shore? It's a sunny, cloudless day." Rosie looked around. There was nothing obstructing their view of the riverbank.

"It gave him a job so we didn't have to bring him with us." Rowdy laughed. "I vote we pretend we don't see him just to see what he does."

"You're a very mean overdressed man." Cinco turned the boat and headed upstream. "I'm in."

Lefty's arm flapping turned panicked as he jumped up and down.

"Why is he running in a serpentine pattern? We're not shooting at him." Worth laughed as he worked his smartphone out of his back pocket. "I have got to get that on video."

"Okay, I'm going to turn around. Everyone stare straight ahead and ignore him." Cinco turned the boat around and headed downstream. "I can't wait to tell CanDee about how much we're messing with Lefty. She'll be so pleased."

"I haven't seen moves like that since the last time I took in a show in Vegas." Rowdy pulled out his smartphone and snapped off a couple of pictures.

"Come on, y'all are going to give him a heart attack." Dallas tried to sit up. "Can we get there already? My ankle is killing me."

"Since when are you a party pooper?" Worth nodded toward Rosie. "He must be trying to impress you." He sat back and looked down at his brother. "I'm just glad you're able to speak in her presence now. That drooling was embarrassing."

"Drooling?" Cinco perked up. "I didn't hear about any drooling."

"Me either." Rowdy shook his head. "I hate when they do that twin bonding thing and don't tell the rest of the world what dumb stuff they've done. So annoying."

The Zodiac touched ground, and Lefty rushed to meet them.

"I'm so glad I was here to wave y'all in or y'all might've ended up in Fredericksburg." He was out of breath. "If I hadn't had them flags, y'all couldn't have seen me."

"Thank you, Lefty, you saved our lives." Rowdy was all grateful solemnity. He hopped off the boat and gave Lefty a big hug.

"Y'all was messing with me, weren't you?" Lefty knew the Rose boys too well.

"No." Rowdy kept his arm around Lefty. "You saved our lives."

Lefty took a step back and regarded them all with his one eye. "Every single one of you besides Rosie here is on my list. No golf carts for a month."

"Hey, what did I do?" Dallas threw his hands up. "All I did was get hurt, and I'm getting punished for something I didn't do."

"You might not be responsible for this one, but I figure you done lots of other stuff." Lefty turned his good eye on Dallas. "Want to tell me what happened to the south fence on the back forty acres when you was in high school?"

Dallas looked around like a cornered rabbit. "One month without a golf cart sounds fair."

"That's what I thought." Lefty threw the flags down and offered Rosie his hand.

"Thank you." She took his hand and stepped off the boat and then turned around to see if she could help them off-load Dallas.

A beep... beep... beeping noise came from higher up the riverbank, like a garbage truck backing up. An ambulance appeared out of the tree line and stopped. The back doors opened and Lucy hopped out. She ran to Dallas.

"An ambulance... really?" Dallas looked at his mother like she'd lost her mind.

Gingerly, she touched his ankle, moving her hands up and down the injury.

The driver of the ambulance got out and walked toward them. "What do you think, Dr. Rose?"

She pointed to Dallas's ankle. "See the gross deformity? I think we're talking talus and tib fracture and maybe some ligament damage.

"Don't you think an ambulance is overkill?" Dallas winced as his brothers laid him down on the riverbank.

"No, I think it's just about right." She smiled down at her son. "We'll need to remove this duct tape and take some X-rays, but I'm pretty sure you're having ankle surgery."

"I don't think that's necessary." Dallas gritted his teeth as his mother touched the top of his ankle.

"How's your pain level?" She continued her examination.

"It wasn't too bad... until now." His face was turning red with the effort of holding back the pain as Lucy explored his injury.

Rosie had to do something to help, only she didn't know what she could do. She knelt beside him and took his hand. "I ran out of ibuprofen this morning, so I'm sure he hurts."

This was all her fault but she couldn't think of a way to fix it.

"It's not that bad." Dallas was breathing heavily and sweat had broken out on his upper lip.

"Can you give him something for the pain?" There had to be something that Lucy could do right now.

"I have something in my bag." Lucy pointed to the ambulance.

A second EMT walked around from the passenger's side of the ambulance and grabbed a black messenger bag. She brought it to Lucy.

Lucy opened it, pulled out a vial and a syringe, and filled the syringe. "This should put a big dent in the pain."

She grabbed a small square packet, ripped off one side, pulled out the alcohol swab, and rubbed it on Dallas's upper arm. She sank the needle into his arm and pushed the plunger.

Lucy looked in the direction of the EMT who'd brought her the messenger bag. "Bev, let's get an IV started. Saline only."

"Yes, Dr. Rose." Bev jumped to attention and ran back to the ambulance. She pulled out a stretcher and tossed a red canvas bag on top. She and the other EMT rolled the stretcher over.

Bev set the red bag on the ground. "Mike, you take his left and I'll take the right." She pointed to Dallas's left. "On three." She bent low, slid her arms under Dallas. "One—"

"Are they really going on three?" Dallas's words were beginning to slur. "It's not like before." He tried to wink at Rosie, but he just kept blinking. At least, she thought he was trying to wink.

"He's stoned... right?" Otherwise he'd suffered a head injury when Rosie wasn't looking.

"Oh yeah. He feels like he has several margaritas in him." Lucy nodded as she looked back at Rosie. "Want me to record all of the goofy things he says on the way to the hospital?"

"No." Rosie shook her head. "Wouldn't be fair."

Worth squatted down next to Rosie. "Why not? I think it would make a wonderful entry for *America's Funniest Home Videos.*"

Dallas waved at Rosie. "Hey, Rosie Posy."

She waved back.

"Shhhh." Dallas shushed everyone and tried to put his

index finger to his pursed lips but he ended up shushing his nose. "No one tell Rosie I'm in love with her, okay? It's too soon. It'll make her uncomfortable."

All eyes turned to Rosie. She had no idea what to do.

He loved her? It did make her uncomfortable. What was she supposed to say?

Dallas blew Rosie a kiss. "She doesn't love me yet, but she likes my body."

Lucy clamped a hand down on Dallas's mouth. "Let's get him to the hospital."

"Yes, I think that would be best." Rowdy put a gentle hand on Rosie's shoulder. "Why don't I drive you over to my house? CanDee and Justus are chomping at the bit to make sure you're okay. Also, your sisters are there waiting for you. It took all of us to keep Louisa from diving into the river and coming to get you."

Louisa was worried about her? Rosie couldn't remember her oldest sister ever worrying about her before.

Things had changed in the time she'd been with Dallas. Hopefully they had changed for the better.

18

osie didn't know how she felt about Dallas going to the hospital without her. Yes, she felt responsible for what had happened to his ankle, but that wasn't it. She really needed to make sure he was okay.

Rowdy opened his truck door for her, waited for her to climb in, and then closed it. She clicked her seatbelt and sat back.

Dallas was in love with her?

She had no idea what to do. This changed things between them... or did it? He hadn't exactly been himself when he'd told her, so maybe she should pretend it never happened.

But what if he really was in love with her? If she pretended that it hadn't happened, wasn't that the same as leading him on?

Rowdy climbed behind the wheel and started the engine. "I bet you're wondering what you should do now."

Since the first day she'd met Rowdy, he'd felt like a brother to her. Come to think of it, so had Cinco.

"I... um..." She took a deep breath and let it out slowly. "I got nothing."

"The way I look at it, you have three options. You can talk to him about it—obviously, when he's not medicated. You can ignore it and pretend it never happened. Or you can run away." Rowdy was Mr. Levelheaded today. "Somehow that last option doesn't seem like you."

"You're right. I'm not going to run away. It's not in my nature to hide from something like this." In that way, she was the opposite of her mother, who'd wanted to hide from everything that was unpleasant. That explained, to a certain extent, her mother's drug use.

"Do you have feelings for him?" Rowdy's tone wasn't accusatory. He was merely asking a question.

"I don't know. I think there's a possibility that I could develop deeper feelings for him, but I'm just getting to know him. Heck, up until a few days ago, he ran out of the room every time I entered it." Dallas could mean a lot to her, but she wasn't sure she was there yet.

"Dallas is a fun-loving guy and always the life of the party, but he also feels things deeply. If you can't return his love, promise me you'll let him down gently." Rowdy kept his eyes on the road. "I know it's a lot to ask, and I know that right now you're overwhelmed, but he's my annoying little brother. He irritates the crap out of me but I don't want him hurt."

She'd never willingly hurt anyone, especially not Dallas.

"I'll do my best." What else could she say?

"I'm sure Justus and CanDee will have better insight into how you should proceed with Dallas." He turned onto the gravel path that led to his house. "I must say that Dallas is going to be so embarrassed when he remembers what he said to you." He sounded like he would enjoy being a fly on the wall when Dallas figured it out.

"You have very strange relationships with your brothers." Rosie knew she had strange relationships with her sisters, but it was nothing like the Rose brothers.

"Speaking of siblings, your sister Louisa is very intense. She and Cinco hit it right off. Two intense stick-in-the-mud people. Their superpower is boring people to death. Louisa's saving grace is amazing flan; unfortunately, Cinco has no redeeming qualities." He hit the garage button on the visor, and the garage door rolled up.

Louisa, Ariana, Esther, CanDee, and Justus were lined up waiting for her.

Rosie's shoulders shook with laughter. "I keep imagining Louisa in tights and a cape. It's so bad."

Rowdy's face twisted in disgust. "Know what's worse? Cinco in tights and a cape."

The image of lanky, seven-foot-tall Cinco in tights and a cape topped off with a cowboy hat popped into her head. It was funnier than her image of Louisa. "Now I can't get that picture out of my mind."

"Welcome to my world." Rowdy stopped the truck just in front of the garage and threw it into park.

Rosie barely had the door open before she was pulled out of the truck and into Louisa's arms.

"We were so worried. You scared us." Louisa held on tight.

"Let me see her." Ariana pulled her out of Louisa's arms and held her out for inspection. "She looks too thin." She looked over at Esther. "Doesn't she look too thin?"

"Leave her alone. She's fine." Esther pulled her into a hug.

Rosie couldn't remember the last time they'd hugged

her. How could she never have noticed that they worried about her? They loved her and they cared for her. They wanted nothing in return. How could she not have seen that before?

"Are you okay?" Justus waited her turn for a hug and then pulled her in. She whispered, "Spoke with Lucy, we'll talk about Dallas later."

"I'm fine. Thanks." Rosie was grateful that she didn't have to tell Justus or CanDee what had happened.

"Okay, it's my turn." CanDee pulled her in. "We were so worried about you."

"I know. I'm so sorry." It was terrible that she'd worried so many people.

"You're fine and that's all that matters." CanDee kept her arm around Rosie as they all headed toward the house.

"Louisa has been cooking all day. She made arroz con pollo and green chili tamales." Justus stepped on the other side of Rosie and put her arm around her friend. "Everyone's staying at our house. Your sisters are spoiling Hugh and AG. It's going to take weeks to beat the Gomez out of them."

"Children should be spoiled." Louisa nodded like it was a law of nature. "I'm teaching Hugh how to make my chocolate flan."

"Hugh said something about food trucks coming in to Roseville to hand out food." Her sisters had helped people out before, but Rosie didn't think she'd ever seen them do anything on this large of a scale.

"Yes, we called several vendors we do business with and everyone was happy to help." Louisa held the door to the kitchen open for everyone. She shook her head. "The devastation is terrible."

"So many people have lost their homes." Ariana hung her head. "Whole families are now homeless."

"We have two families staying with us." CanDee followed Rosie into the kitchen.

"There's a family staying in your cottage, Rosie." Justus followed close behind. "We moved your things into a bedroom here. I hope you don't mind."

"Of course I don't mind. It was the right thing to do." Rosie found herself being led to the kitchen table by her two best friends.

Louisa went to the stove. "Do you want arroz con pollo or tamales first?"

"I'd love a shower and a change of clothes and then some arroz con pollo." Rosie didn't want to sound ungrateful, but she needed to get to the hospital. Dallas would be having surgery, and she needed to make sure he was okay.

"I'll get the food ready while you take a shower." Louisa pulled out plates and utensils.

"Let me show you to your room." As Justus pointed in the direction of the hallway, she shot CanDee a look that said, "Follow us."

With CanDee on her right and Justus on her left, Rosie made her way down the hallway to the very last door on the left. Justus opened the door for her, waited for CanDee and Rosie to walk inside, and then followed and closed the door.

"Dallas told you he's in love with you." Justus leaned against the closed door. "Spill."

"I don't know what else to say. Lucy gave him an injection for the pain and he told everyone not to tell me that he's in love with me." Rosie set her work tote down on the bed. "I don't know what to do."

"You don't have to do anything." CanDee plopped down on the bed. "Please tell me you had sex with him."

"A lady never kisses and tells." Rosie grinned.

"Since when? Talking about sex is what distinguishes us from the other animals. Well, that and really great shoes." CanDee grabbed Rosie's hand and tugged on it until she sat next to her.

"We did and it was amazing." Rosie couldn't help the smile on her face. She'd really enjoyed her alone time with Dallas.

"So you found the condoms I packed?" Justus sat on the other side of CanDee.

"Yes, and thank you for the yoga pants and T-shirt." Rosie didn't know what she would do without her friends.

"You're welcome. I snuck those in at the last minute. Men are so stupid, all they wanted to pack was the sat phone, some beef jerky, a compass, and a waterproof flashlight. I lost the battle for clean underwear." Justus shot Rosie a cheeky grin. "I packed a dozen condoms, how many are left?"

"A dozen?" CanDee looked at Justus. "That's wishful thinking."

Rosie held up four fingers. "Only four left."

"How do you feel about Dallas professing his love?" CanDee watched her very carefully.

"I don't know. I have feelings for him, but they're new. I think love is a possibility... one day. I'm not sure I'm there quite yet." Rosie didn't want to call it quits with him, but she wasn't ready to jump into anything serious. "I like him. I enjoy spending time with him. I'd like to get to know him better, but for now, that's all I have to offer."

"That's enough for now." CanDee patted Rosie's knee. "Just keep an open mind."

Justus shook her head. "Not sure how you're going to bring up the subject with Dallas, but I know you will. If there's anyone in the world who faces challenges head-on, it's you." She bent forward to look around CanDee. "Now that you're back, I can't wait to see how you organize the rebuilding of our B&B and also the benefit concert we'd like to put on to help the victims of the flood." She shot Rosie a sugary sweet and totally fake smile. "See how I threw that last bit in there? We were hoping you'd volunteer to organize the concert... will you?"

"Of course." Organizing was her middle name. She would put together the best damn benefit concert ever.

"Good, because we already told everyone you'd do it." CanDee grinned at Rosie. "Your sisters are organizing the food. I knew your sisters were a force to be reckoned with, but now I see where you get your organization skills and your work ethic. Those three women could run the world with one hand tied behind their backs."

It was Rosie's turn to smile. "I know. I'm thankful they've taught me so much."

"You should have seen Louisa." Justus shook her head. "I thought Lucy was going to have to sedate your sister to keep her from trying to swim across the river. I've never seen anything like it."

"I called them as soon as we got your call on Tuesday night. They were here an hour and a half later." CanDee's eyebrows bounced off her hairline. "Just thought you should know that."

"How's that possible? Austin's almost three hours from here." Her sisters never broke the speed limit... ever. Rosie had always felt there was a wall between her and her sisters. She knew they loved her, but she'd thought it was out of obligation. She needed her friends' take on it. "Do you think my sisters regret taking me in?"

"No," they said unison.

"I've always felt that I owed them because they took me in." Rosie traced the zipper of her work tote. "Dallas got me thinking that maybe the feeling of obligation I have toward them is all on my end. I mean, I know they love me, but I've always felt that I had to work harder than everyone else so they wouldn't regret all they've given up for me."

"First, you told Dallas about Izora?" CanDee gritted her teeth like the name left a bad taste in her mouth. She and Justus always called Rosie's mother by her first name because they refused to refer to her as anyone's mother.

"Yes." Rosie had actually told him more than she'd ever shared with anyone.

"Second, your neurosis over love coming with big, thick, choking strings comes directly from Izora. From an early age, she made you believe that you were worthless and that the only thing that could make you worthwhile was hard work." CanDee caught Justus's eye. "What did she used to ask Rosie? It was something about justifying her existence."

"It was, 'What have you done today to justify living?' That is evil and I hope she's burning in hell." Justus hated Rosie's mother almost as much as CanDee hated her.

The bedroom door burst open and Louisa walked in. "I can't believe that—that *bitch* said that to you."

Rosie didn't know what to do. She'd never heard Louisa this angry. She'd never even heard her curse.

"Girls," Louisa looked at CanDee and then Justus, "I apologize for listening at the door, but I need a minute with my sister."

"Okay." CanDee stood, grabbed Justus's hand, and pulled her into the hallway.

Louisa sat down beside Rosie. She took her hand. "First, I need to apologize to you for not taking you away from her sooner. I was young and stupid and turned a blind eye to what was going on."

"We all did." Ariana stepped into the room, followed by Esther.

Esther sat down on the other side of Rosie. "I think we were all so happy to have gotten out of the house that we didn't think about what was happening to you."

Ariana knelt in front of Rosie. "If you want to tell us how bad it was, we're here to listen. If you'd rather not talk about her, that's fine too. We're so sorry for leaving you there for so long."

"This may be a terrible thing to say, but our mother overdosing was the best thing that ever happened to you—" Louisa's voice cracked, so she cleared her throat. "It's the best thing that could have happened to us."

"Wait a minute. Mom didn't OD, she had a heart attack." Rosie remembered the heart attack. It hadn't been an overdose.

"She OD'd. The coroner put heart attack as the cause of death because Mom had a small insurance policy that wouldn't pay out if she OD'd. He was being kind, and it wasn't a lie. Not really. She did die of a heart attack, but it was caused by the overdose." Ariana put both of her hands on Rosie's knees. "We didn't tell you the truth because we wanted to spare you. You had been through so much, and we didn't want you to be hurt by her anymore."

"We are so sorry that you had to live through hell with her. We really didn't know how bad she'd gotten." Esther's voice was pleading. "We've never been anything but proud of you and happy you came to live with us. If it hadn't been for you, I don't know where we'd be today. You gave us the kick in the pants to make something of ourselves. It wasn't easy, but look where we are now."

"I'm so sorry if I ever made you feel like you owed me anything." Louisa shook her head. "I never meant for that to happen."

Tears burned Rosie's eyes. "I always felt like I needed to work harder and longer to make you proud of me, but a friend pointed out to me that you probably didn't feel that way, that it was me."

Ariana pulled a wad of tissues out of her pocket and handed them to Rosie. "Even from the grave, our mother can still hurt you. Too bad she can't die twice." She sounded furious.

"Rosie, we have never been anything but proud of you." Louisa pulled her in for a hug. "When you first came to live with us, you were so sad. We didn't know what to do. I'm not much of a touchy-feely person, but I guess I should have tried harder. You needed that and I should have given it to you."

"No, no," Esther said. "It was me. I should have spent more time with you." Now she was crying too. "When we got the call that you were trapped on the other side of a flooded river, we all lost it. We can't lose you. You're our finest accomplishment. The only thing our mother did right was have you."

"Did you know that when she was pregnant with you, we used to play with your little feet?" Ariana smiled at the memory. "You would kick out through her tummy and we'd push back. It made you kick harder. After you were born, we took turns watching you. You were so tiny and sweet."

"I never knew that." Rosie had had no idea that her sisters loved her so much. No, that wasn't it. She'd never let herself see how much her sisters loved her because she'd been too caught up in the mental and physical scars left behind by her mother's abuse. That ended today.

Rosie wiped at her eyes and stood. "I hate to run out so soon, but I've got a shower to take and then a hospital to visit."

"Dallas Rose is a hottie." Esther grinned. "His twin's cute too."

Louisa pushed Esther playfully. "Worth is a good ten years younger than you."

"So, he's still cute." Esther grinned. "I haven't had a date in so long, I can't remember. How about you put in a good word for me." She winked at Rosie.

"I'll see what I can do." Rosie hugged each of her sisters in turn.

Now that she looked back on her life with her sisters, she could see how much they loved her.

Knowing that they loved her and wanted her in their lives made her heart full.

19

Dallas woke up in a light-green-painted room and couldn't remember why he was there. People were moving around and machines buzzed in the background. He glanced at the IV line dripping something into his arm. Hospital. He was in the hospital. Something about his ankle.

Oh yeah. Rosie had been in trouble and he'd made sure she was okay. He'd broken his ankle crossing the river.

He smiled to himself. He and Rosie had gotten along really well. The sex had been amazing, and the time they'd spent together had been even better. Where was Rosie?

"Hello, Dallas, how are you feeling? I'm Lorraine, your recovery nurse." The woman who spoke was short and had wiry gray hair and eyes that matched the light green walls. "Any nausea, blurred vision, or headache?"

"No." He looked around. "Did I have surgery?" His thoughts were fuzzy. Hadn't his brothers come in a Zodiac to get Rosie and him? "Where's Rosie?"

His mother appeared at his side and pulled a chair up next to the bed. "She's in the waiting room with every other member of our family and hers. They brought a lot of food and have set up a tailgate of sorts in the waiting room." She sat beside him. "How are you feeling?"

"Good, I guess. I'm really tired and my head's a little fuzzy." He vaguely remembered telling Rosie that he loved her. Had that really happened or had he dreamed it? God, he hoped he'd dreamed it.

"We'll get you into a room shortly. Your ankle was pretty bad and because we couldn't get to it sooner, your body had already begun healing it, which made it more complicated to fix. Anyway, you're going to be out of commission for a while."

"How out of commission?" It was a broken ankle. How bad could it be?

"You'll be on crutches for at least six weeks." She stood and patted his hand. "I'll get you moved and then you can see Rosie." She turned to walk away.

"Mom." He reached for her hand. "Did I tell Rosie that I was in love with her or did I dream that?"

"Do you want the truth or would you like for me to tell you what you want to hear?" His mother grinned down at him.

"Crap. It wasn't a dream." How in the hell was he ever going to be able to face Rosie again? A week ago he'd have said that not being able to talk to her was the worst thing in his life. Now he wished he hadn't been able to talk to her.

His mother bent down and said next to his ear, "At least she didn't run screaming back to Austin. She's still here and anxious to see you. That means something."

He didn't want to pin his future on false hope, but at the moment he didn't have anything else to pin it on.

Thirty minutes later, he was wheeled into a hospital

room. He'd be staying overnight but could hopefully leave in the morning.

Rosie walked into his room, followed by Justus holding AG, Hugh holding a huge bouquet of flowers, and three Hispanic women he'd never laid eyes on.

Rosie went to his bedside and sat in the chair his mother had pulled up to the bed. She took his hand and nodded in the direction of the door. "These are my sisters. Louisa, Ariana, and Esther."

He wished he could stand and meet them properly, but the best he could offer was a smile and a handshake.

He shook Ariana's hand. He knew she was the middle sister because of what Rosie had told him.

She grasped his hand warmly. "We've heard a lot about you. Thank you for risking your life to make sure she was safe."

"It was my pleasure." He glanced at Rosie, who winked at him.

Louisa, the oldest, was next. She shook his hand and then leaned over and whispered, "Rosie has a pretty big crush on you. If you break her heart, I'll kill you slowly."

She stood back up and glared down at him.

Louisa was exactly like Rosie had described. "Understood." He would give every cent he had to be alone with Rosie. She had more than a crush on him. She had a "pretty big" crush on him. His soul smiled. It was more than he could have dreamed. She'd told her sisters about him. It wasn't just the pain meds making him outrageously happy.

The last sister, Esther, held her hand out for him to shake. She pumped his hand twice and then dropped it. She made a V with her index and middle finger and then brought them to her eyes in the universal I'm-watching-you gesture.

"Uncle Dallas, I brought you some flowers." Hugh walked to the bed and proudly presented the huge vase of flowers.

Justus handed AG over to Louisa and pulled the small tray table over and set the flowers on top. "We don't want to keep you. We just wanted to make sure you were okay." She leaned down and kissed him on the cheek. "We have to go now. Lucy is only letting us in to see you in small groups."

Christ, there were more people for him to see? All he wanted was some private time with Rosie and maybe a bacon cheeseburger and fries. Right now, it didn't look like his chances were too good of getting either.

All of his brothers filed in and then out, followed by Lefty and CanDee and his father. Several of the ranch hands came to pay their respects, as well as Pastor Green and his wife. All in all, there were too many people keeping him from Rosie.

An hour and a half later, the last visitor waved goodbye and headed out the door.

"I thought we would never be alone." He brought Rosie's hand to his lips and kissed it. "So, you have a pretty big crush on me?"

Beating around the bush was for subtle people, and Dallas didn't do subtle.

She gave him a peck on the lips. "No, sorry, you were misinformed."

His whole world turned sad and dark. All of the spit dried up in his mouth. What was he supposed to say and do now? She'd told him at the Villa that she cared about him, but maybe she'd changed her mind.

"I don't have a big crush on you. I'm in love with you." She clamped a hand over her mouth and looked like she was replaying her last sentence over in her head trying to figure it out. "I didn't mean to say that out loud."

Everything turned sunny and bright again. "Yes, but you did say it, and I heard it, and there's no take-backs. Sorry, but those are the rules. You're officially in love with me."

Her eyes were huge, and it looked like she was still processing what she'd just said. "I'm, um... I'm in love with you." She sounded... well, kinda mad.

He wasn't sure how to take that.

She bit her bottom lip. "I'm in love with you?" Asking it didn't do much for his ego.

She sighed. "I'm in love with you." This time she'd stated it, which was better. "It's too soon and I never do anything impulsive, but I'm in love with you."

"I'm in love with you too." He couldn't wait to see what would happen next.

"I'm in love with you." This time it came out easier. "I want to get married and have a family." She clamped her hand over her mouth again. "I think I need to stop talking right now."

"If you'll remember, I asked you to marry me at the Villa. I just want to point out, you didn't say no." He was enjoying her discomfort. It was petty and childish but it was also comforting that she was in this with him. Love had made him a drooling idiot. Now it was her turn.

"I thought you were kidding." She looked like she was replaying the conversation in her mind. "I'm sure you were kidding."

"Was I? I believe we agreed on a simple wedding with just family and a few friends. Outdoors under a blue, sunny, cloudless sky." He'd paid attention.

"But... it's too soon." She sounded like even she didn't believe that.

"Why? I've been in love with you since the day I walked into Rowdy's kitchen and first laid eyes on you. I loved you then and I love you now. I'll love you forever, always–evermore."

"You're just saying that so you can score some hospital sex." She kissed him lightly.

"I'm not going to lie, it did cross my mind." He brought her hand to his lips and kissed it again. "We could start making those babies now." He made a big show of checking the clock on the wall opposite him. "I've got nothing but time."

EPILOGUE—TWO MONTHS LATER

Rosie buttoned the last of the tiny little silk-covered buttons on the back of CanDee's antique-white wedding dress. The dress was a simple sheath that was cut low to show a good amount of cleavage.

"I can't believe today is finally here." CanDee turned around to look at herself in the full-length mirror on the back of the bathroom door. Even though she'd had the dress fitted before she knew she was pregnant, it still fit perfectly.

Rosie glanced around the bathroom. It was the one and only bathroom in the old Victorian house CanDee and Cinco shared. If one had to live with only one bathroom, this was the bathroom to have. A seventeen-head shower took up the whole back wall. A marble bathtub big enough to swim in took up a good chunk of the right wall, and two substantial pedestal sinks took up the left.

"You're the last one of us to get married." Justus tilted her head to the left like she was trying to puzzle it out. "How did that happen? It feels like you've been engaged forever."

"I know... right?" CanDee stared at herself in the mirror. "Is it time for the veil?"

CanDee was using Cinco's great-great-aunt's wedding veil.

"Yes, it's almost ten forty. The guests started arriving almost an hour ago." Rosie walked to the window at the back of the shower. "Looks like most everyone is seated."

Today, she wasn't a wedding planner, she was a bridesmaid.

And yesterday, she'd been a bride. She and Dallas had tied the knot in the front yard of the Villa with just a few family and friends in attendance. It had been a perfect day.

Their wedding gift to each other had been the Villa. It had been the place where they'd fallen in love, and now it would be their home.

"Give me a hand." Justus nodded to the veil. "It's so fragile."

Rosie picked up the end of the veil's long train, and she and Justus walked it over to CanDee. Justus bobby-pinned it on the top of CanDee's head.

Rosie smoothed down the train.

The bathroom door eased open, and a head with lots of fluffy gray haired peeked in.

It was CanDee's grandmother. "There's my beautiful girl."

"Come in, Grammie." Justus waved her in.

In true Grammie style, she was wearing an unconventional mother-of-the-bride purple lace top and purple leather pants. Rosie had to give it to the older woman, she did things her way, even if it was hard to watch.

Grammie pulled a small black velvet box from behind her back. "This was my grandmother's. She gave it to my mother on her wedding day and then it came to me. Now it's your turn." She opened the box, and a beautiful sapphire and diamond pendant glittered in the overhead lighting.

She unhooked the pendant from the velvet-covered clips and placed it around CanDee's neck.

"It's so beautiful." CanDee's eyes teared up so she fanned her face. "I'm going to cry and my makeup's going to run.

"If you cry then I'll cry." Justus fanned her face too.

"Not us." Grammie put her arm around Rosie. "No sympathetic crying here."

"That's because you two are emotionally challenged." CanDee took the tissue Justus offered.

"I prefer to think of it as emotionally guarded." Grammie waved her hand. "All of that emotion's too much trouble."

There was another knock at the door, and Lefty's head poked around the door. His eyes locked on Grammie and his shoulders went back. "Lois, I didn't know you were in here."

She sauntered over, pulled him into the room by his lapels, and gave him a big smacking kiss on the lips. "Last night was fun."

Lefty blushed a deep red.

Rosie had never seen a man blush quite that glowing shade of red, and she hadn't expected it from an old, ornery, rough-and-tumble cowboy.

"Yes, it was fun." His eyes were glued to Grammie's.

A thought struck Rosie. "I didn't know your name was Lois. I don't think I've ever heard anyone use it."

"I'm Grammie to most people and Hot Stuff to others." She hip-bumped Lefty. "Did you see my Harley parked out back?"

"Yep, but it's missing a seat. I ain't never seen no motor-cycle that didn't have no seat." Stiffly, Lefty put his arm around Grammie. "I could fix it for you."

"That would be nice." Grammie put her arm around

him. She was a good four inches taller than Lefty. "I'm always happy to trade sexual favors for work."

Rosie and CanDee gagged in unison.

Rosie might not be overly emotional, but her gag reflex worked just fine.

"You two are such prudes. I think it's nice that they found each other." Justus picked up CanDee's bouquet.

"If you're so open to it, how would you feel if your dad and stepmom talked about their sex life in front of you?" CanDee looked a little green.

Justus thought about it for a minute. She gagged. "I stand corrected."

A string quartet started up.

Rosie checked the time. It was ten forty-five. "They're right on time."

CanDee went totally still and leaned closer to the closed door. "Is that Katy Perry's 'Roar'? Who even knew there was string quartet sheet music for that?"

"You agreed to let Cinco pick out the wedding music." Rosie smoothed out the wrinkles in her peach racer-back bridesmaid's dress. The deep orangey-pink complimented her olive skin. "It's time."

"Okay." Grammie kissed CanDee on the cheek. "I love you, kiddo."

"I love you too." CanDee smiled at her grandmother.

"I need to go get my seat." Grammie patted Lefty on the butt. "I'll see you later." She slipped out the door.

Rosie checked her watch again. "We need to head downstairs."

Lefty offered CanDee his arm. "If I'd had a daughter, I would have wanted her to be just like you."

CanDee took hold of his arm. "Thanks for walking me down the aisle."

Lefty held out his other hand like he wanted to shake hands. CanDee took it and yelped.

"I got you, I got you, I got you," Lefty sing-songed as the unicorn glittered on the eye patch covering his right eye. He waved around the buzzer he'd had in his hand so that everyone could see it.

"Good one." CanDee leaned down and gave him a peck on the cheek. "You got me."

Fifteen minutes later, Rosie walked down the aisle on the arm of her newly minted husband.

Dallas whispered, "Are you sad we didn't do something like this?"

"Not even a little. I enjoyed our small ceremony. I didn't miss the pomp and circumstance a bit." She glanced up at him. "How about you?"

"Are you kidding? I'm wearing a tuxedo. Nobody in their right mind wants to wear a tuxedo." He winked at her. "I love you."

"I love you more." She winked back at him.

"How about you show me later how much you love me?" He waggled his eyebrows.

"You're on."

He looked down the front of her dress.

"Stop looking down my dress." She elbowed him ever so slightly.

"It's a date, Rosie Rose." He loved using her new name.

"I really should have thought that out before I agreed to change my last name." It was a terrible name, but she didn't care. She wore it proudly.

"Sorry, no take-backs." He blew her a kiss as they parted in front of the minister and went to stand on their respective sides.

He eye-flirted with her through the whole ceremony.

She loved the way that he loved her—without reserve... without limits... without the expectation of something in return.

ABOUT THE AUTHOR

Katie Graykowski is an award-winning author who likes sassy heroines, Mexican food, movies where lots of stuff gets blown up, and glitter nail polish. She lives on a hilltop outside of Austin, Texas, where her home office has an excellent view of the Texas Hill Country. When she's not writing, she's scuba diving. Drop by her website, www.katiegraykowski.com, or send her an email at katiegraykowski@me.com.

Made in the USA
Middletown, DE
15 March 2023

26728111R00109